The Mission

'Earth!'

The Emperor nodded.

'You want me to go to Earth?' said Cora.

The Emperor nodded again.

'You can't send me to Earth. I won't go.' Her eyes narrowed as spikes of anger shot towards her uncle.

'Cora, Cora,' said Emperor RAMcoat, 'we have no choice –'

'Choice? Choice?' she said. Her voice was almost a squeak.

'Will you please stop repeating everything I say?'

'But the Commander is going to destroy that planet . . .' Cora's voice faded as a wary look crossed her face on its journey towards disappointment.

'We don't know that for sure yet,' the Emperor reminded her.

'But the Commander said –'

'I know what the Commander said. But the truth is we don't have all the facts to decide whether it should be destroyed.'

'We have the most important fact,' Cora said, glaring at him. 'They're murderers.'

The Emperor slowly shook his head. 'Go and find out for yourself,' he said quietly.

'They killed my parents. Your own sister. Isn't that enough?'

The Emperor sighed. 'Just do this one thing for me, that's all: go and see for yourself.'

Cora's face was like stone. Her eyes widened as his words sunk in. She stared at her uncle without blinking. 'I'll go if you agree to abide by my decision,' she said.

The Emperor's brow furrowed. 'Um, well –'

'Will you abide by my decision?' Cora's words growled from the back of her throat, rumbling at the Emperor.

'OK.' He sighed again. 'If there's no other way you'll go.'

'What about the language? I don't speak their stupid language.'

'It's not *the* language. There are actually 7106 languages on Earth.'

She rolled her eyes.

'We'll just update your ROM with English. That's the language they speak where you're going.'

'And what do these weird aliens look like? she said. 'How am I supposed to blend in with them?'

'They actually look a lot like us.'

Cora raised her eyebrows. There was a moment's silence before she continued. 'I take it Commander HardDrive from the Space Fleet will be coming with me?'

'I was actually thinking of someone else,' said the Emperor. 'Someone who might blend in better with the locals.'

Cora's eyes locked onto his. 'Who?'

'Your best friend.'

'Loopy? Just Loopy and me?'

He nodded.

Her mouth dropped open. She was finally speechless.

Princess Lucinda was sprawled on the couch, her eyes closed and her face turned towards the window. The red sun hung in the morning sky and its pink rays warmed her face. Her mouth felt slightly dry but she was too comfortable to move.

'Loopy?'

She ignored the voice.

'Loopy!' It was more insistent now.

'Go away. I'm having a nap while the place is quiet,' Lucinda said.

'Loopy . . .' This time the tone was low. A warning.

One brown eye opened wide, expecting to see the voice's owner, Commander HardDrive, wrapped in her red space suit. But that's not what it saw. It saw a shimmering, moving cluster of particles. They were there, but they weren't there.

She wasn't that surprised. It took a lot to surprise Loopy. She closed her eye again. 'What?'

'I've got something for you,' said the Commander.

'I'm not hungry.'

'Don't be ridiculous, you're always hungry. But that's not it.'

Silence.

'I've brought you an upgrade.'

Both eyes shot open. Four paws scooted her off the sofa. Loopy stood to attention before the iridescent particles. Some particles broke off and rearranged into a shiny collar.

'Iridor?' Loopy smiled. 'The same as Cora's eyes. My favourite colour.'

'Try it on,' said the Commander.

More particles formed into an arm and hand. Fingers reached out and removed Loopy's red WooFi collar and fastened the new one around her neck.

'Now you've got an enhanced connection to the Super Loop Operating System,' said the Commander.

'Wow, the power of SLOS!' said Loopy. She tilted her head as she turned towards the cluster of Commander.

A bowl of water shot across the room and was caught by the cluster hand.

'What was that?' said Loopy.

'Ah. You've just found one of your new skills. You can cause inanimate objects to move. I take it you were thinking about getting a drink?'

'Collikinesis' whispered Loopy, wide eyed.

'Your extrasensory skills are clearly also stronger too – that's exactly what we called it!' The Commander laughed. 'It sounds like a comedy Earth word. They have a certain flair for stating the obvious.'

'Earth?' said Loopy. 'Why are you talking about Earth? Am I going on a mission?'

'Yes, with Cora.'

'What's the food like there?'

'Loopy, can you please stop talking about food for one minute!' .

Loopy grinned. 'What equipment does Cora get?'

'Well, we thought it would be best to just leave Cora as she is with the ROM in her hat for now. The Emperor and I discussed it and we think that Cora is still a little bit, um . . . too unpredictable at the moment to handle upgrades.'

'You mean she's stroppy.'

Commander HardDrive laughed. '*Impulsive* sounds kinder, Loopy. And you'll need to mind your speech on that planet,' she said. 'They're not as advanced as we are. Animals don't speak there.'

'What? Don't speak? I don't like the sound of that much.' Loopy studied the swirling particles. 'I can see you've mastered nanotechnology transport.'

The particles spun into a dark-haired woman in a red space suit. Arms folded, she tapped the toes of her right foot on the ground.

'Yes, I'm having fun trying it out. What do you think, Loopy?' she said.

Loopy nodded approval. 'It's good. Am I to presume this means you can reassemble anywhere in the universe?'

'It's still a work in progress,' said the Commander. 'And, Loopy, remember – mind your language!'

She reached down and patted Loopy's soft collie fur. There was nothing else in the universe that felt like that.

As she straightened up, Commander Amander HardDrive broke into a billion pieces of swirling iridescent particles and faded out of sight.

The Arrival

Carrickfergus was experiencing its typical weather: drab and misty. As a whirring sound faded into the distance, a cool wind picked at the ends of the golden-brown hair of a young girl who stood on the grass. A slight shiver moved through her slim body.

'Is this it?' she said.

There was no answer.

'Loopy?'

'Mm?' came a distracted response, followed by a few sniffs.

'Where exactly are we?'

There was silence for a moment while Loopy waited for her link to the Super Loop Operating System to make the connection. They were, after all, a *very* long way from home.

'Yes, according to SLOS we are in Northern Ireland.'

'North-ern Ire-land.' The girl rolled the words around her tongue, trying out the sounds in the strange new language provided by her ROM. 'Ire Land? The Land of Ire? Ire as in "anger"? Huh! They only think they're angry. I'll show them anger!'

The girl glanced down at the black and white collie standing by her feet. The dog's head was knee high and her fur was gently ruffled by a wind that also made her ears wobble.

Loopy looked up at Cora, sniffed again and wrinkled her nose.

This place smelled really bad. Like wet, dead stuff.

Cora dragged her gaze through the morning mist that hung like a ghostly shroud over the land. It came to rest on a huge stone building with coarse grey walls.

'Is everything grey here?' she said.

Loopy didn't bother to answer. She really didn't care that much for this place or whatever colour it might be for that matter.

Below the building's giant tower was an arched door half hidden behind a thick wooden gate.

'What is that?' Cora said, glancing at the iron bars in the windows.

Loopy looked up in surprise. Cora was actually showing interest in something.

'Um, SLOS says it's an important place, um. . . Norman castle.'

'Is that their emperor?'

'Who?'

'Norman.'

'I don't know. The SLOS connection is lagging,' said Loopy.

Cora turned her gaze from the building to a flat area where many metal objects in different shiny colours were lined up. They had wide glass windows, wheels and flattened roofs. They looked like mutant spacecraft.

'What are those?' She nodded in their direction.

'Transport vehicles, I think. The signal's not picking up very well yet.' Loopy shook her neck in an effort to improve the WooFi link to SLOS. 'Remember, they don't fly on this planet,' she said.

'Primitives,' Cora mumbled. 'Well, Emperor Norman has a lot of vehicles. He must be a powerful ruler.'

Loopy looked towards the long streak of dark water behind

the castle. 'That's Belfast Lough. It runs into the Irish Sea.'

A light, tuneless clanging carried through the air.

'Those things making the noise with the pointy bits sticking up are *boats*,' said Loopy. 'For transport on water.'

Wide-eyed, Cora turned in the direction of Loopy's gaze. 'What? Humans don't swim either?' she said. 'What kind of weirdos live here?'

The dark ocean oozed towards the castle walls, clutching at it with wet fingers before dragging them back again into the crawling mass of water. The tip of Cora's tongue swept a thin film of salt from her lips. There was a strange smell. Rotting vegetation? Not unpleasant, just strange.

Her attention was caught by a bright globe on a slow journey up from the horizon, sending a watery, shimmering light across the ocean. She realised it was the sun in this solar system *Yellow*. It was slightly mesmerising. So different from SLOI.

She lowered her eyes, swallowing the lump in her throat. She felt alone, even with Loopy for company, here on this far-flung world, light years from home. If she could even call SLOI home any more. She loved her uncle very much but it wasn't the same since her parents died. It didn't quite feel like a real family.

The moment passed and she straightened to her full height, which was about average for a thirteen-year-old girl.

'Right then. Let's get on with it. We have a mission to carry out,' she said. 'I don't want to hang about here any longer than I have to. She glanced back at the grey castle and grey sidewalk. This place is already giving me the creeps.' The corners of her mouth turned downward as she turned up her nose. 'The Emperor should have just listened to what the Space Fleet Commander said.'

'Maybe.' Loopy hesitated. 'But . . .'

'But what?'

'But don't you think that the Commander is a bit harsh?' Loopy said.

Cora's eyes blazed as she swung her head towards her friend. 'Harsh? How can you say that?' Her voice broke. 'This mission is just a waste of time. You know as well as I do what these people are capable of. I would have annihilated the whole lot of them three years ago if you ask me.'

Loopy did not reply. She was worried. Because that's exactly what the Emperor would be doing – asking Cora. And as much as Loopy loved Cora, she had to admit this was not the type of decision that should be made by an angry teenager who, it seemed, had already made up her mind.

The Land of Ire

The pair walked in an awkward silence. Cora wondered what had caused Emperor RAMcoat to chose this dreary grey place. Did he even have a reason? Why here? What was so special about this place for such an important mission? Anyhow, she supposed he must have had his reasons so they'd better have a good look at this place and try to figure out what the Earthlings were really like.

Loopy blended in very well with the locals. Cora realised that the Emperor had chosen well to send her. A few people had already wandered past with different types of dog. She had seen a particularly cute brown curly-haired one. They seemed to have leads attached to their collars that their human held onto. However, there were some that may or may not have been actual dogs. Small hairy things. They looked more like sontor. *Slippers* her ROM told her. At least Loopy looked like a normal black and white collie dog, even though the WooFi in her collar could access the most advanced information system in the universe and its iridor colour was invisible to the Earthling eye. She wondered what it might look like on their spectrum. Green? Blue? Violet?

Cora tried to look inconspicuous as they wandered through the town, like any girl just out for a walk with her dog. She almost succeeded in her long-sleeved T-shirt, plain black skirt and stripy tights. Her clothes might have seemed a bit warm for a summer anywhere else, but fitted in here in Northern Ireland. There was a little bit of a problem with her legs, though. They were inclined to wobble and jerk in an odd manner. Sometimes they seemed to make random movements on their own, at other times they seemed to not want to move at all.

'Their gravity is quite a bit stronger than I thought it would be,' she whispered to the now silent Loopy. Her gravity boots weren't helping as much as she had expected. Although they had been adjusted to Earth's gravity it was taking a few minutes to get the hang of walking. The clumpy black boots themselves didn't look too bad – she could see they were similar to the boots worn by some of the locals – but they felt like they were being wrenched back to the ground by a big magnet of too much gravity.

Her knitted black hat had a slightly pointed tip. It was equipped with a read-only-memory lexicon holding translations of SLOI words, but there were some things on this planet that had no Sloian equivalent. Like the metal thing with two wheels that a young boy perched on as he rolled past them on the walkway. It was very odd. Cora glanced at Loopy, remembering that she had been well warned not to reply if there were Earthlings around. She wished her hat had a direct link to SLOS like Loopy's collar did so that she could get more information. Maybe she could get an upgrade. She wondered why she hadn't been given one. Anyone would think Emperor RAMcoat didn't trust her.

As they strode along the walkway, she began to notice that the hat was drawing odd looks and smirks from passers-by.

Before Cora could figure out why, two girls sauntered towards her. One had long frizzy blond hair and Cora could see she was wearing strange blue gel on her eyelids. She also had ridiculously long eyelashes compared to the other people around. In fact, her skin didn't appear normal either. It seemed rather orange. As Cora looked at her she realised that the rumour must be true that aliens really did come in strange colours. The girl was wearing some kind of garment that was so tight it looked like it had been sprayed on. She wondered if it might be a form of nanotechnology, but decided not. Even the Sloians hadn't mastered that yet. Well, not as far as she knew.

The orange-frizzy-blond girl's companion had cropped dark hair. It was sticking out in little pokes all over her head. She had a metal ring through her nose and she obviously had no eyebrows as she had drawn a pair on with a black pen. She wore a short skirt with no tights and her chalk-white legs had a distinct tinge of blue from the cool morning air. Little bumps were standing out on her skin.

Both girls were chewing something, clacking loudly, their mouths opening and closing like faulty electronic shutters.

Orange-frizzy-blonde stepped right in front of Cora, blocking her way.

Cora tried to move around her but Nose-ring Girl stepped up beside her friend. She sneered at Cora.

'Where you goin' in yer charity-shop clothes, weirdo?' she said.

Both girls sniggered.

Cora wasn't exactly sure how to respond. What on Earth was a charity shop?

'Let me past, please.' She said it politely, keeping her voice calm, looking Nose-ring Girl directly in the eye.

'*Let me past, pleeeeese . . .*' mocked Orange-frizzy-blonde, wiggling her head from side to side, still clacking away at the chewing gum. Her mouth stretched wide in an evil grin, revealing oddly dazzling white teeth.

Without warning, Nose-ring Girl grabbed Cora's hat and whipped it onto the darker stone area by the walkway, where the wheeled-vehicles whizzed up and down.

Wheeled vehicles whizzed towards it.

Cora's emotions battled for control. She was briefly puzzled – why would this girl do such a thing? – but then fury won the battle, and Cora worked hard to keep it under control. Her mum had given her that hat. It was her most precious possession. She never ever went anywhere without it.

'Whaccha gonna do now without your wacky weirdo witch hat?' sneered Nose-ring Girl. Orange-frizzy blonde gave a snorted laugh.

Cora swallowed the lump in her throat. *I am not weak,* she reminded herself. *I am* never *going to be vulnerable again.* She wasn't afraid. Knowledge is power and she had knowledge coming out of her hat. Literally.

Moreover, she also had another type of power. These idiots didn't know what they had just done. She needed to be careful, though. One word, that's all it would take. Just one word to Loopy and the connection to SLOS straight to Commander HardDrive and this planet's fate would be signed, sealed and delivered. It would be goodbye Earth. *Adios. Au revoir. Sayonara. Arrivederci. Auf wiedersehen.* Whichever one of their 7106 languages they chose.

In her peripheral vision she saw Loopy leap into the vehicle area. There was a loud screeching noise as a wheeled thing swerved sharply to avoid the collie and an infuriated driver yelled out the window.

Cora just about had time to wonder again why these Earthlings always seemed so angry.

Loopy – her agile, acrobatic, loyal best friend – grabbed the hat and leaped back to the walkway. Loopy was safe. The hat was safe. Now, where were they?

Cora tilted her head slightly, blinking slowly. She looked at her tormentors. She folded her arms and leaned heavily on one leg. She sighed. Really these bullies were nothing more than an inconvenience.

'Oh, so ya think yer better than us, do ye?' said Nose-ring Girl. She spat her gum directly at Cora. Missing its target, it fell to the ground.

Quick as a flash, the girl grabbed a handful of Cora's hair, swinging her to one side. Her tight grip was painful, pulling at Cora's skin. Then, pushing hard with her free hand, she shoved Cora sideways, almost causing her to overbalance.

These girls were no strangers to fighting in the street.

Loopy stood on alert. Watching. Holding her emotions tightly in check. Just waiting for one signal from Cora.

Pulling back slightly, Nose-ring Girl swung her leg to deliver a kick in Cora's direction.

Loopy continued to hold back, hardly breathing.

Cora stopped dead still.

Okay. That was it. Enough was enough.

She snapped her fingers.

Nose-ring Girl's leg locked in mid-air, triggering a sharp pain to her right hip and causing her to tumble as she released her grip on Cora. She crashed onto the pavement in a heap, banging her face on the edge of the kerb, loosening a tooth. There was a metallic taste in the girl's mouth. Blood. She gulped, then swallowed the wobbling tooth.

Cora looked down at her and smiled sweetly. 'Don't worry,

you'll see that tooth again in a couple of days,' she said.

'Ya rotten cow!' Nose-ring Girl shrieked, as her orange-frizzy-blond sidekick tried to haul her off the ground. 'I don't know what ya did there. I knew ya were some kinda wacky weirdo witch, so ye are. I'll git ya fer this.' She shoved Orange-frizzy-blonde hard on the shoulder, resisting her help.

'Oi! I was just tryin' t' help ye!' yelled Orange-frizzy-blonde, her face turning an angry shade of puce. It really didn't suit her any more than the orange.

Cora rolled her eyes as her two attackers began to fight with each other. She reached out to Loopy, took her hat and firmly placed it back on her head. 'Thank you, Loopy,' she said. 'What exactly happened there?' Her expression was calm but her heart was pounding.

Loopy grinned. 'Collikinesis,' she said.

The two girls were so busy screeching, slapping, spitting and scratching each other that they never even noticed as Cora began to walk away.

'What is wrong with these people?' Cora wondered aloud. 'They don't even know me, yet they just attacked me. And what on Earth is a witch?' She sighed. 'It seems my hat is drawing attention to us,' Cora said to Loopy when they were out of earshot. 'I refuse to take it off, though. You'll need to make it invisible.'

Loopy nodded. 'Okay, that's the hat screened,' she whispered.

Cora reached up to gently touch it. 'I can still feel it.'

'I know, but no-one can see it,' whispered Loopy.

Cora breathed a sigh of relief. She loved that hat. If those girls had damaged it they would have been really sorry.

They might still be, she considered. Them and their hateful, angry planet.

She didn't notice that the girls had stopped fighting. Or that the air bristled with hostility as they watched her walk away.

Food for Thought

'Look what I see, Loopy,' said Cora.

Loopy looked up from inspecting an empty can at the side of the road. A smile lit up her face. Their pace quickened from a stroll to a march.

The corners of Cora's mouth turned upwards too. She loved it when Loopy smiled. It was like someone had switched on the midday sun. It was impossible to be grumpy with that collie for long.

The travellers followed the footpath past many strange-shaped buildings. Nothing else around them was familiar, but Cora had seen what she thought were myra, waving leafy branches in the distance, beckoning them closer. Her ROM told her that on this planet they called them *trees.*

The myra on SLOI were a vast array of colours. It was a very beautiful planet. These Earth trees had brown trunks and the leaves were only green, even though there were many different shades. Her ROM told her there was a saying in Ireland that there were forty shades of green. In her opinion it really didn't matter how many shades of green there were, they would never be as pretty as the ones on SLOI. For some reason the trees were imprisoned behind heavy black iron gates, but the gates were at least open, so Cora and Loopy walked on through.

Cora heard Loopy whisper the word *park.*

A man was pushing his toddler son on a wooden seat with ropes attaching it to a metal frame. There were two others exactly the same beside it but they were empty. He glanced in their direction, but then turned back to the child, not really that interested in the young girl and her dog.

Cora glanced at him, wondering if he was Emperor Norman.

The grass had been freshly cut and a sweet scent wafted from the bushes. It seemed to come from the ones with the soft spirals of velvety petals.

Cora stopped. These were like the lupran that grew on SLOI but she had never seen them in this particular shape before.

Reverently she reached out and touched the petals. They reminded her of the smoothness of her mother's skin. Her eyes blurred, even though the fragrance was beautiful. Loopy told her the Earthlings called them *roses* but to be careful because even the most beautiful ones sometimes had vicious thorns.

Cora looked up at the clusters of myra that stood as straight as guards on sentinel duty. Then she chose a bumpy mound of grass and flopped down. She rested her back against a wide trunk of gnarled brown-grey bark. Its branches stretched out like arms reaching towards the sky. Towards home. The curl of the myra leaves seemed like smiles at the sun. Cora thought it was quite pretty, for a plain green tree.

Sprawling at Cora's side, Loopy began to gobble up stringy stalks and blades of grass, whipping them swiftly through the air. She also unearthed clods of soil, white roots, the lot – in an effort to gobble up as many mouthfuls as quickly as she could before Cora's restlessness moved them on their way.

Munching and gulping the grass, Loopy could hardly contain her excitement when she noticed some slinky, slimy, slithery worms that had been unearthed in the soil. She snapped one

Chloe

The snap was quickly followed by a rumbling, vibrating snarl and ended in an ear-splitting, '*WOOF!*'

A large dog poked its face through the gate at the bottom of a garden. It growled ferociously, shaking its head as if trying to rupture the bars of the gate. Huge German Shepherd incisors were bared. Tall ears pricked straight up. Fur stood on end.

Loopy's head spun as fast as if she'd been called for dinner. Wide-eyed, she looked at the creature. 'Good grief! What is that?' she said.

'Um . . . I think it's some kind of dog,' said Cora.

Loopy was indignant. 'Don't be so insulting, Cora. Look at its primitive aggressive response. It's not exactly very bright, is it?'

As soon as Loopy's eyes had locked onto the would-be predator, it yelped and leaped back from the gate. Although its four legs were rigid and its ears were still standing to attention, its eyes were stretched wide and its tongue lolled out of one side of its mouth.

Loopy could not decide if it was afraid of her. It should be. Perhaps it was just daft. She raised a pair of collie eyebrows. *Nitwit*, she thought. This time she knew not to speak aloud as a small female Earthling had appeared from behind the gate.

'Sorry 'bout the dog. She's a bit barmy. Skippy – behave!'

The voice belonged to the little girl. Dark curls swung as she shook her head crossly at the dog, but her green eyes shone with fun.

The dog grumbled a complaint, snorted, then clumped itself down hard on the ground. She crossed her front legs, tilted her head to one side, and plopped her chin on her front paws, resting her nose on the ground. Big brown eyes looked up at Cora and Loopy. She'd gone for cute, but letting them know that she was still alert and watching.

'She thinks she's so brave but she really is the most scaredy dog you will ever meet. It's even hard to believe she's a German Shepherd. I'm Chloe,' said the girl, in a tumble of words.

An amazed Loopy watched Cora smile gently at the little Earthling.

'Hi, I'm Cora, and this is my dog Loopy.'

The little girl laughed. 'What a funny name. Why do you call her Loopy?'

Cora could have replied that this most special of dogs was linked into the Super Loop Operating System, one of the most advanced technological systems in the universe. Instead she just said, 'She's a bit crazy, so I call her Loopy.'

A pair of collie eyes gave Cora a disapproving look.

'Well, actually my mum named her Lucy. Although I called her Princess Lucinda.'

Chloe laughed.

'I was only three at the time,' Cora said. The memory brought with it a sad smile.

Loopy looked up in surprise. She couldn't remember the last time Cora had smiled. She seemed to like this little girl in the rubber boots with blue dungarees and yellow T-shirt. Loopy thought she looked around eight Earth years old. Perhaps Cora had smiled as the clothes were streaked with mud and grass or maybe it was the red blotches on one side of her face. She did look cute.

'I was just picking some strawberries. Would you like some?' asked Chloe, holding out her hand.

'Um, what do you do with them?' asked Cora.

'You *eat* them, of course, silly,' said Chloe, giggling again. She tilted her head to one side as her forehead folded into a frown. Obviously Cora was a bit odd.

'Oh,' Cora murmured. She very cautiously raised a strawberry to her lips, inhaling the wonderfully fruity smell – a scent as strong as the aroma of the freshly cut grass they'd just snacked on and the roses they'd found.

She noticed that the strawberry things were growing in the garden on a leafy plant with a grassy type of stalk attached. That probably meant they were okay to eat.

Chloe eagerly popped a strawberry into her mouth and began chomping. She grinned widely, her teeth coated in red mush. She wiped the dribble at the side of her mouth with the back of her hand, smearing more red goo across her face.

Not wanting to be impolite, Cora gingerly took a bite. Her eyebrows lifted in surprise as she marvelled at the soft, juicy yet firm strawberry fruitiness. Loopy watched carefully through eyes as round as the hubcaps on the car in the driveway.

'Loop, you've got to try one of these,' Cora said.

'She eats fruit?' said Chloe.

'She eats mostly anything,' said Cora.

Chloe slid her small hand through the gate and held out a strawberry to Loopy. Loopy took it very gently, careful not to hurt the little girl's hand, not caring that the hand was covered in muck. Loopy was well used to muck as she could often be found rummaging for food in all sorts of unsavoury places. She quickly scoffed the strawberry then looked up at Cora, rewarding her with the biggest doggy smile she had ever seen.

'These are wonderful, Chloe. Thank you,' Cora said. She decided that these strawberries were much tastier than her usual diet. She'd definitely never seen these on SLOI.

'Can't believe you've never even had strawberries before. Where on Earth have you *been* all your life?' said Chloe, stretching out both arms and raising her palms upwards.

Cora smiled sweetly at the irony and gently reached down to stroke the fur on Loopy's head. She thought that collie fur was the softest, smoothest, sweetest, most wonderful thing in the universe.

Two big brown eyes watched from the driveway. Skippy grumbled to herself. She was put out by the collie – *Princess Lucinda*, if you please – who clearly thought she was the best thing on four legs. Chloe was *her* pack, and no collie was going to paw her way into Chloe's heart and –

Suddenly a fly passed by and obliterated her train of thought.

Skippy jumped up and trotted across the grass. Her head cocked to one side, then the other. Her eyes locked on, hypnotised by the buzzing.

The fly swirled and flew, dropping, swooping – up, down, around and around. *Buzz, buzz.* Swirl, swirl. Skippy followed behind it, tail wagging as lightly as a flag in a summer breeze. Her eyes were alert and her teeth snapped as she missed every time. This fly was an expert navigator but on a good day this garden was definitely a no-fly zone.

The fly suddenly swerved towards the fence and Skippy

launched herself into the air in a final assault, but the fly quickly changed direction and flew the other way. Unfortunately it was too fast and Skippy continued to soar through the air until her head connected with the fence in a loud *whuuuump.* She crumpled to the ground.

'You almost knocked yourself squiffy, Skippy,' said Chloe. She laughed. 'When will you ever learn? Even the flies can outwit you!'

'Grrrr,' grumbled Skippy, looking somewhat embarrassed.

Suddenly she swung her head towards Loopy, ears alert. She could have sworn that she heard the word *nitwit* in her head, but the collie was innocently just standing there, minding its own business.

Suddenly a loud rumbling and rattling vibrated from the direction of the back garden.

Skippy leaped up and scrambled towards it. She slithered along in an avalanche of paws, slipping and sliding in her haste, tail wagging madly, and barking wildly.

Chloe laughed again. 'Slippy Skippy!' she shouted after the dog. 'It's the lawnmower,' she told Cora.

'Lawnmower?' By the puzzled look on her face, Loopy knew Cora didn't have that word in her lexicon as they didn't have lawnmowers on SLOI. She couldn't understand why they just hadn't given Cora a link to SLOS like she had. Anyone would think they didn't trust her. Did they think she was going to hack her way into the Command Centre and launch a missile or something?

'Yes, when anyone starts a lawnmower she literally goes barking mad. She charges along behind it. She slides all over the place, chomping the grass, flinging it in the air, jumping up and down. Her feet even turn green.'

'Green?' said Cora, wondering if jumping up and down on this planet made your feet turn green. She wondered if the girl with the blue legs was inclined to jump up and down. Blue and green are right beside each other on the spectrum. That would explain a lot.

'Yeah, Sappy Skippy. The sap from the cut grass soaks into her fur and her feet go completely green. Like an alien. Or a leprechaun.'

Cora smiled. She knew what an alien was, although she'd never seen a green one. She wondered why this girl thought aliens were green when some of the ones on this planet looked orange. But a leprechaun? She had no idea what that was. It must be some other kind of alien, though Cora had never heard of it. It definitely wasn't from SLOI. She realised she liked this little girl and her silly jokes. And her comic dog.

In the back garden, Skippy suddenly stopped. Ears up, head cocked to one side, tail up straight. Alert. And all because she could have sworn she heard a mocking voice in her head saying, 'You're turning into a leprechaun, nitwit.'

Unsure how to continue the conversation, Cora nodded at a nearby sign for the zoo.

'Um, where is the zoo?' she asked in the hope that the chatty Chloe would explain what it exactly it was as well. She reckoned it must be important if there was a sign showing the Earthlings where it was.

'It's not far. You like animals, don't you?' continued Chloe.

'Is there anyone who doesn't?' Cora's eyes narrowed as she frowned, suddenly serious.

'Mummy, told me that some people don't deserve to have animals because they are cruel to them.' Chloe's eyes flashed as green as a ballistic missile.

Cora wondered if Nose-ring Girl and Orange-fuzzy-blonde liked animals. She decided it was unlikely. They bullied even people who looked different – what chance would poor, defenceless animals have? Well, apart from Loopy, she was certainly not defenceless. She had the connection to Commander HardDrive who could explode this planet into a gazillion pieces.

She realised her mind had wandered off when she heard Chloe speak again.

'Are you going to the zoo?' Chloe asked. 'I'm going up there later. My cousins work there in the school holidays. My uncle is the boss.'

'He's in charge?' said Cora, listening to her ROM's translation. 'Like an emperor?'

'Um, maybe.'

'Is his name Norman?'

'Um, no, it's Sam. Sam Ryan,' said Chloe, somewhat confused. When Cora didn't say anything, she blethered on. 'There are loads of different animals there. It's where they all live, you know.'

Cora was silent for a moment more. An emperor. In his own kingdom. This could be very important. And you could always learn a lot about people by how they treated animals. She decided she'd better check it out.

'Okay then, Loopy.' Cora smiled at her collie companion. 'It looks like we're off to the zoo.'

'It's just up that way a bit. Just go straight and you'll see another big sign, and you're there,' said Chloe, flapping her hand vaguely up the road.

'Okay, Chloe,' said Cora, 'we'll keep a look out for it. I hope I'll see you again some time,' she added. She was surprised to realise that she actually meant it.

She turned a thought over in her mind.

Could she really destroy a planet when it had people like Chloe living there?

Not everyone was like Chloe, though. She'd just arrived and had already seen that first hand. Surely one small person couldn't make much difference in a world full of murderers and bullies.

It was a matter of weighing things up she supposed. The lesser of two evils.

Chloe was very sweet.

But Earthlings were definitely evil. There was no denying that.

The Zoo

It turned out that the zoo was easy to find. The travellers had already been more than halfway there.

When they came to another big sign, a few drips and splatters of water fell from the sky. Loopy said that the dripping water was called *rain* on this planet. SLOS said it was extremely common in Northern Ireland, even in the summer, and that sometimes it went on for months on end.

They watched a woman cross the busy road at some flashing lights and they copied what she did.

'SLOS says the zoo sits on the side of the Cavehill mountain,' whispered Loopy.

'Is the mountain a hill with caves in it?' said Cora, rolling her eyes. These Earthlings really had no imagination.

They walked up a steep and winding path that led them into a grey area where many cars were parked. Cora wondered how many of them belonged to Emperor Norman.

'Ha ha,' said Loopy. 'Look, that sign says "Zoovenir Shop".'

Cora ignored her. She had no idea what a zoovenier was meant to be. Then she noticed something worrying. A brown wooden hut with a flat roof and a glass window displayed a large sign. It instructed, PAY HERE.

Cora reached into her pocket. She had no money, but her fingers closed around a plastic disc the Commander had given her. Never having used it before, she warily approached the window.

She leaned forward to peer into the semi-dark interior. There was a greasy-haired, scraggy man hunched over a desk. He looked up and slowly untangled himself from the chair. His wiry frame was wrapped in a manky shirt with sweaty circles under the armpits. His crumpled grey trousers, held up with a frayed black belt, stopped abruptly at the top of once-white-now-grey sports socks. His huge feet looked like they'd been shoved inside shoes two sizes too small, causing the scrunched up socks around his ankles to look like like dirty tennis balls.

He shuffled grudgingly towards the window and scowled.

Cora took a step back as an unpleasant aroma assaulted her nose.

The man scratched his grey stubble and the drip on the end of his nose plopped to the ground.

Cora's eyes widened. An unpleasant taste made itself known at the back of her throat.

'Yesss?' the man hissed. His dire grimace revealed pointed yellow teeth with brown stains. He'd clearly been told to smile at customers, but Cora really wished he would stop.

'Um, we'd like to come in,' said Cora, holding up the disc. The Commander had told her it should display what Earthlings expected to see and would help her out of difficult situations.

The man peered at it through rheumy red-rimmed eyes and sniffed loudly. She could hear the mucous rattling its way up his nose and down into his throat.

Gross, she thought. This was her first close-up encounter with an adult Earthling. Were they all like this? Her stomach contracted, forcing the debris at the back of her throat further towards daylight.

'Humph,' he grumbled. '*You* can come in but *that thing* can't.' He pointed a bony finger with a broken yellow nail to where Loopy stood. 'No dogs allowed. Tie it up,' he instructed, flicking his hand towards the gate.

'No, you don't understand. I'm not leaving her – we're together.'

'Take your pick, girl,' he said, rasping through a slimy cough. 'Either it stays out or ye both stay out.'

Cora's face crumpled. 'Skorbot,' she exclaimed. The man gave her a sharp glance before turning away. She didn't understand how someone could be so unkind, especially someone who worked at a zoo. It was no wonder that Commander HardDrive wanted to annihilate these Earthlings. They were vile. Obviously the Commander wasn't harsh at all!

Cora swung on her heels and stomped off. Loopy followed closely behind, keen to get away. She was having serious reservations about how that man had smelled. She was sure there was something very unsavoury about him.

Cora knew there was no way she was going to leave her best friend behind. She wondered why Chloe hadn't told her that dogs weren't welcome in the zoo. Her face was a puzzle of consternation as she flounced back towards the parked cars. If this man's nasty attitude was an example of how humans treated animals then she really needed to see inside this place. That should be more than enough evidence for Emperor RAMcoat.

Suddenly Loopy's ears pricked up and she looked towards the Zoovenir Shop.

'Cora,' she whispered. 'I think someone's trying to get your attention.'

Cora looked up and sure enough there was a tall boy with curly reddish-brown hair lurking by the shop, just out of sight of the entrance gate. He beckoned them over. Loopy thought he might be around fifteen Earth years but it was hard to tell as he seemed taller than some of the adult Earthlings they'd seen.

The boy wore a green T-shirt with the zoo logo printed under a small, embroidered grey barneygore. Cora smiled when she recognised it. Her ROM told her they were called *elephants* on this planet. His trousers were blue and streaked with mud and goodness only knew what else, although Loopy thought she could tell from the smell. On his feet were a pair of heavy boots, not unlike Cora's.

'Never mind him,' said the boy, nodding towards the ticket office. 'That's Rob Snufflebot. He's vile. We were short-staffed today. He's a temporary replacement. Last minute. We didn't really have much choice. It was either him or M'Granny. But he definitely won't be back tomorrow.'

Cora nodded, unsure what to say.

'Do you want to come in? I'm about to do the food for the tapirs and chimps.' His friendly hazel eyes looked thoughtfully at Loopy. 'Could your dog sit quietly in the barrow?' He beckoned towards a wheelbarrow stuffed full of chopped fruit and vegetables. 'We could hide her under a blanket.'

He could have sworn the dog gave a slight nod but decided it was his imagination.

'Oh, thank you. That would be great. My dog is very well behaved,' said Cora. She glanced at Loopy. 'Well, mostly.'

'Okay,' said the boy. He pushed as much of the contents of the barrow as he could to one side.

Cora tapped the empty side of the barrow. 'Okay, Loop, in you get.'

Loopy jumped into the barrow and lay down quietly. The boy

gently covered her with a slightly grimy but soft yellow blanket normally used for animal bedding. He'd left enough of a gap so that she could see out over the side.

Loopy was somewhat disgruntled. A wheelbarrow was hardly a befitting carriage for someone of her importance, but given a lack of options, she wriggled around and settled herself in. When she did, her opinion quickly changed – she noticed the smell. An alert gleam appeared in her eyes. She could smell – well, stuff. It smelled good. It smelled good enough to eat. Well, really everything smelled good enough to eat where Loopy was concerned, but this smelled kind of earthy and fruity, like the strawberries they'd had earlier. Her job at the moment was to wait quietly so, in spite of the urge to investigate further, she sat still.

The boy lifted the handles of the barrow and wheeled it forward. It was heavily weighed down by its freight of food and dog. Although the wheel at the front squeaked and crunched over the ground, the boy held it steady.

They hiked the short way towards a sign that said, TAPIRS. Cora didn't know what a tapir was, and she was very curious. The lexicon didn't offer a translation, so it seemed like they didn't have that species on SLOI. Loopy, frankly, wasn't that bothered. She had other things on her mind.

'It's quiet at the moment,' the boy said. 'Most of the visitors have gone off to have afternoon tea.'

Loopy decided she'd like to have some afternoon tea. Whatever that was. It sounded like something to eat.

Cora followed the boy into an indoor enclosure where another young boy, with brown eyes and hair so shiny and dark that it almost looked blue, was waiting. He was dressed in the same uniform except that the pockets of his scruffy blue trousers appeared to be stuffed with various unidentifiable objects.

'Oh, hello,' he said. 'I'm Andy. I see you've met my older bother.'

'Ha ha, very funny,' the boy with the barrow replied. He turned to Cora and said, 'Sorry, I should have introduced myself. I'm Eoin Ryan. That's my *brother* Andy. Armed and dangerous!' He pointed to the catapult hanging out of one back pocket and a Swiss army knife in the other. 'The last time I checked he was also carrying three pens, string, a biscuit, half a packet of chewing gum, a used postage stamp, a piece of squashed up Blu Tack and various sweetie papers. Mum has great fun when she clears out his pockets to wash his trousers.'

Cora laughed. It seemed the brothers liked to tease each other. She knew how brothers behaved, although she didn't have one herself, unfortunately.

'Don't worry, O-wen,' she said, pronouncing his name as it sounded to her ears. 'I think we were all a little distracted back there. I'm Cora, and this is Loopy.' She peeled back the blanket to reveal the black and white furry face with madcap eyes and a wet nose.

The Ryan brothers laughed.

'You both have really strange names,' remarked Eoin.

'Yeah, almost as strange as yours,' Andy teased. 'His name is spelled E-O-I-N.'

'Oh? Why is that strange?' Cora said.

'It's the original Irish spelling,' Eoin informed her. 'And my brother thinks he's a comedian. A comedian with pockets full of weapons and food,' he added. 'Cora's not a very common name. I've never actually met anyone called Cora before. What's your surname?'

'ROMhat,' she said cautiously.

'*Romhat?*' Eoin questioned. *Cora Romhat.* He had a feeling he'd heard the name before somewhere but couldn't quite remember where. 'ROM as in a computer's *read only memory*?' he asked, smiling.

Cora tried to stop her eyes from widening as best she could. She had not expected this. This boy was smart. Could Eoin have picked up the Super Loop connection? Could Earthlings understand a biologically based hardware interaction? No. No way – she'd grown up with it and she could only just about get her head round it.

She said nothing.

'Does that mean you can never change your mind?' joked Eoin, smiling again.

'Ha.' Cora laughed shakily. 'My memory is my memory. It's permanent. Only new experiences can be added.'

The boys looked at each other. They weren't exactly sure what she meant by that. She seemed a bit odd.

Monkey Business

'We've a new baby here, Cora,' said Andy. He swung open the gate to the tapir house. Cora's eyes widened in astonishment when she saw the four-legged, rough-haired animal.

'I've never seen one of these before,' Cora told him.

'Yeah, they look really odd, don't they? Kind of like a pig crossed with an elephant.'

Cora's lexicon told her that was a kind of snuffler crossed with a barneygore. The dark grey animal looked as though it had sat in a tub half filled with white paint, though its hind legs were still grey. Its nose was a cross between a snout and a trunk and it had three giant toes on each foot. Cora decided it was quite a lot like a small version of a barneygore. The animal eyed Cora nervously before sauntering over to Andy. She nuzzled his hand.

'This is the mummy, Tania,' said Andy, 'and over there is Tina.'

Cora's gaze followed the direction of Andy's pointed finger and there was a very strange sight. She had thought the mummy tapir was odd, but the baby was even more so. Although Tina's shape was a miniature version of her mummy, her coat had very peculiar markings of random white, wobbly stripes and dots. Cora thought they were like a drawing done by a small child with a shaky hand. Maybe Chloe. It made her smile.

As Loopy jumped out of the barrow she noticed that this smiling business was becoming a bit of a habit since their arrival on this planet.

Eoin stepped forward. 'Okay, let's get them fed,' he said. He began to pick up handfuls of food from the barrow and drop them down near the tapirs.

Loopy had identified the chopped-up food as a mixture of apples, carrots, twigs, small branches, leaves and a selection of berries. Quickly looking around to see if anyone was watching, she edged her way towards a few pieces of apple that had slipped from Eoin's hands. With the speed of a ninja warrior, she snapped up a slice of apple and chewed quickly before she was spotted. She was delighted to find it extremely flavoursome – just as nice as Chloe's strawberries. Juicy yet firm, with a wonderful tangy aroma. As she looked for another piece she realised that grass and worms were actually quite boring.

When the tapirs were fed, Eoin said he had to feed the chimpanzees, and asked Cora if she would like to go with him. She nodded. He was surprised when Loopy jumped back into the wheelbarrow without being asked and waited to be covered with the blanket. Andy opened the door and Eoin wheeled the barrow back outside. With Cora at his side, they began the hike up the hill to the chimpanzee house.

When the odd trio arrived, Cora recognised the species immediately. They were called moon-keys on SLOI. Some Sloians even believed that they had evolved from them. Yet, here they were on Earth. Odd. She'd need to think about that a bit more later.

'Would you look at that?' exclaimed Eoin through gritted teeth. 'People are throwing food to the chimps, even though the sign clearly says not to.' Red-faced, he stomped forward into the crowd of visitors.

'Please! Just STOP that, will you?' he shouted, scowling into the crowd.

People's heads turned to look at him in amazement, as if he'd just said he was going to build a spaceship out of ice-cream and fly to the moon in his underpants.

'Loop?' whispered Cora. 'Can you do anything to help Eoin?' She hated it when people broke the rules. Rules were important. They were there for a good reason.

'Gurrfle ullomm,' came the reply from under the blanket.

Cora looked on helplessly. She could feel her blood boil as some people just clearly ignored Eoin. How irresponsible. She'd like to show them a thing or two. They clearly thought they were so smart.

And then a very strange thing happened. Every time someone threw something at the chimps, the chimps picked up handfuls of poop and aimed the mucky missile in a direct path towards that person.

One particularly defiant teenager who was throwing chewing gum was rewarded by a smack on the side of the head from some sloppy yellowy-brown chimp poop. It stuck to his face and got in his ear and hair. The smell made him start to gag.

He tried to flick it away but then it got on his hands. He began to leap up and down, flicking at his hair and shaking his hands, shouting, 'Eww! Ewwwww! Gross. Get it *off* me!'

Eoin began to laugh. 'Well, you got what you deserve,' he said to the boy, who skulked off with rounded shoulders and a grumpy red face.

'Well done, Loop,' whispered Cora. 'That'll teach them,' she said aloud.

Eoin glanced her way. He didn't say anything, but for a fleeting second his eyes narrowed and a puzzled look crossed his face. 'Come on,' he said, 'let's take the barrow inside the chimp house.'

He wheeled the barrow through the back entrance and lifted off the blanket to let Loopy out.

He noticed that, although Loopy jumped out and shook herself just like a normal collie, she seemed to have a bit of a smirk on her face. He thought he must be going insane. How could a dog smirk? *Why* would a dog smirk?

'We've cut the bananas in two or three pieces cos the chimps eat them so quickly that they're gone in no time,' Eoin told Cora, as he handed over her share. 'Just throw them through the bars.'

Cora threw the pieces in one at a time. One chimp leaped over and grabbed a piece of banana. It crouched down, its bright red bottom brushing the floor as it peeled the banana skin away so that it could pop the fruit inside its mouth. Then it bounced up and down on its haunches, grinning widely, screeching and chomping at the same time.

Cora was enchanted for a moment. 'How cute,' she said. It reminded her of the moon-keys at home, except for one very important fact: on SLOI, the animals were never, ever behind bars. Earthlings didn't seem to have any sense of right and wrong. Why would they keep animals caged up? They had just as much right to be free on their own planet as the humans had.

For however long that might be.

Loopy, on the other hand, had other things on her mind. Well, not really things, just one thing. She eyed some pieces of banana in the barrow and when Eoin and Cora had turned their backs to feed the chimps she quickly snuffled up two pieces, skins and all. She liked it. She liked it a lot. Yes, Earth food was definitely much nicer than the typical SLOI diet.

When the bananas were all finished, Eoin turned to Cora again.

'Cora, I'm sorry but we don't really have any more time to show you around the zoo before closing and we have to keep Loopy hidden from old Snufflebot. Why don't you come back after closing when he's gone?' He pointed. 'We live just over there behind the complex and we can come back in. Dad won't mind, he knows we're sensible.'

'Are you sure?' asked Cora, taken by surprise. This boy must see how much she loved the animals and was willing to bend the rules again for her. She glanced at Loopy, who gave a discreet nod. 'That's really kind, I'd really love to see more of the animals.' It would also give her an opportunity to learn more about these kids. The next generation of Earthlings. And there were things here she really needed to find out about, like why the animals were kept locked up.

'That's settled then. We'll meet you after the zoo closes.'

Loopy jumped back into the barrow and Cora strolled with Eoin to the exit near the Ryan house where Loopy jumped out and they said goodbye. She looked forward to returning to the zoo later. It would be useful to chat with the boys again. She wasn't sure, but she might even have liked them. No. Maybe not yet. But even that couldn't be right. She wasn't supposed to like Earthlings. Was she?

Deep in thought, struggling with confusion, she didn't notice the two beady eyes watching from behind the bushes. And she had no way of knowing that a warped brain was hatching an evil plan.

Flying Apostrophes

'I kind of like the local language. It rolls nicely off the tongue,' said Cora as she and Loopy wandered down the main road. They were taking the opportunity to observe more humans and their behaviour before going back to the zoo. 'It's very descriptive. The sort of language you can really get your teeth into.'

Loopy couldn't reply as there were people around but she gazed at Cora, puzzled. English was descriptive all right but she found that when she was speaking any language she most definitely had to keep her teeth out of it or there would be all sorts of trouble.

A small shiny blue and purple sweet wrapper blew across the pavement. Loopy thought it looked interesting. She didn't know exactly what it was but she pounced anyway. She caught it in her teeth and gave it a quick chew. It tasted sugary-sweet and slightly sticky. Nice.

She gave it another quick chew, then swallowed it, feeling quite pleased with herself. She had captured something tasty.

They came to some shops. There were market stalls on the walkway that were loaded with a brightly coloured assortment of items. Cora recognised crimson apples, ripe bananas and juicy strawberries among them, but there were many other things of various shapes and sizes that she did not recognise. She noticed large orange balls about the size of her hand that had pitted, shiny skin, and something similar in smaller, yellow, oval shapes. There were squishy-looking red balls, each with some kind of a dead green thing with legs on top, and beside them were miniature green trees. Some other things looked like apples with smooth fur.

Cora wondered what all this weird stuff was, convinced it surely couldn't all be human food. Grass and worms was more than choice enough for Sloians.

A handwritten sign on the shop window read, ALL TYPES OF FRUIT'S SOLD HERE. Cora rolled her eyes. By now she had learned enough of the language to know that this was nonsensical.

'Just look at that,' she complained to Loopy. 'Don't they know there's no need for an apostrophe there? And, as if that's not bad enough, the plural of *fruit* is actually still *fruit*. Are Earthlings really that dim that they can't even speak their own language properly?'

Loopy nodded.

Further on they stopped outside what Loopy declared was the local library. It also had a sign. SECOND-HAND BOOK'S FOR SALE.

'Look, Cora,' whispered Loopy, 'another one.'

'Oh, Skorbot.' Cora was exasperated. 'Don't these idiots know you only use an apostrophe when you've dropped out a letter?'

Loopy nodded again.

'Or to show ownership – like "the dog's dinner" for one dog or "the dogs' dinner" for more than one?'

Loopy hoped there was only one dog. She wasn't prepared to share her dinner.

'It seems that they just stick random apostrophes anywhere they see the letter *s*. Honestly, isn't it annoying that these stupid creatures don't even know how to punctuate their own language? They've got apostrophe-itis!'

Loopy was pretty sure that word wasn't in the lexicon. She wondered if it was something to eat. Or an illness. Maybe humans got it if they ate the dog's dinner. It would serve them right.

A young man came out of a big building and placed a sign on the walkway. It read, BISCUIT'S HALF PRICE.

'Oh, Loopy, this is dreadful.' Cora sighed. 'These idiots are destroying their lovely language.'

'I can put it right,' Loopy whispered. She hesitated, knowing that Cora didn't like these Earth people and their nitwit ways. It was unlikely that she would want to help them.

Cora's shoulders slumped as she rolled her eyes. They really didn't deserve any help. 'Okay, Loop,' she sighed. 'Just this once. Go on then.'

Suddenly the sky became dark as every single apostrophe that was in the wrong place soared straight up into the sky from all sorts of places – including signs, newspapers, solicitors' letters, badly written novels, teachers' reports and children's homework. Grammar was suddenly corrected as apostrophes were tugged free, catapulted through the atmosphere, and launched into space where it was already dark and they couldn't be seen.

Now *ALL TYPES OF FRUIT* (Loopy had also extracted the unnecessary s, which at that moment was whizzing past Neptune) were being sold at the fruit shop. *SECOND-HAND BOOKS* were on sale at the public library and *BISCUITS* were half price in the supermarket.

People wandered into the street and looked up in puzzlement.

'Was there supposed to be a solar eclipse today?' one man

asked his wife.

'No,' she replied, 'but that was too quick to be an eclipse.'

After some shoulder shrugging, people returned to their normal activities and quickly forgot about the strange and unexplained dark sky. They were too self-absorbed to even notice that their ridiculous punctuation had been corrected.

Cora had had enough of earth adults. They didn't even notice what was in front of their very eyes. It looked like the children on this planet were much more intelligent. She hoped so for the sake of the planet's future. If it had one.

The Sloian Apostrophe Police headed back towards the zoo. Cora led the way, with Loopy trotting alongside, still snapping up sticky sweetie wrappers that hadn't been placed in a bin.

They had no idea that bad grammar would soon be the very least of their worries.

The Tree House

Eoin stood near the back gate of the zoo. He was playing a game on his mobile phone while waiting for the girl and her dog. He hardly noticed when they approached, and only looked up when Cora stood right in front of him.

'Andy's just coming,' he said. 'He's doing some target practice with his catapult.'

Cora smiled.

'He's really very good,' Eoin continued. 'He can do a straight shot right on target. He has a very keen eye.'

Although the English lexicon in Cora's ROM was excellent, the slang was a bit lacking. She continued to smile politely and nod, but was wondering why Andy might just have one keen eye and what exactly it was keen to do. Shoot the catapult, maybe? But how could you shoot a catapult with your eye?

Earthlings clearly had strange ways of doing things. That much was for sure.

A few minutes later, Andy came running down the road and caught up with them. 'Sorry 'bout that,' he panted. 'Chloe and Skippy are up at the house. They just came up with Aunty Jasmine.'

'Chloe and Skippy?' said Cora.

'Yeah.' Andy laughed. 'She said she'd met a girl with a lovely collie. Was that you?'

Cora nodded.

'Our mothers are sisters,' he said. 'Chloe's really funny. She brings Skippy into the zoo all the time and she even named her after a kangaroo – cos she bounces about a lot. She always calls her daft names like Squiffy. And Slippy. And Sniffy.'

'She's only little but she's actually quite intelligent,' said Eoin.

'And actually quite bossy,' added Andy.

The boys laughed.

'I don't think I've ever seen a kangaroo,' Cora said.

'We have kangaroos here,' said Andy. 'Would you and Loopy like to see them?' He patted Loopy's fluffy head and noticed just how soft her fur was. Even though the zoo was full of animals, he'd never felt fur quite like that before.

'Yes, please,' said Cora. 'Anything that looks like Skippy has got to be worth a look.'

This time it was Loopy who rolled her eyes.

They wandered down to the kangaroo enclosure and Andy strolled up to the fence. He made a whistling sound and a large creature on two legs hopped over. It was huge. Cora's jaw dropped. They didn't have that species on SLOI.

'These are the biggest kangaroos of all,' Andy explained, 'and this one is even taller than Eoin.'

Eoin stuck out his tongue at his brother.

Cora laughed. Again, Loopy observed. A definite pattern.

The kangaroo stood well over six feet tall. It had reddish brown fur, a small head with a longish nose, dark eyes, pointy ears, and a very long muscular tail.

'In this species the males are red but the females and young are usually grey. They come from Australia – a whole twelve thousand miles away,' said Andy.

Cora knew that was close enough to still be on this planet. Somewhere.

'It's quite sad really. Many of these lovely animals are killed on the roads. They're not very intelligent and just dart out in front of traffic,' continued Andy. 'They can cause massive damage to a car.'

'That's not the only sad thing. Andy, I don't mean to be rude . . .' Cora smoothed her left eyebrow with the tip of her index finger. '. . . but isn't it cruel to keep animals locked up like this?'

Andy nodded, a serious expression on his face. 'I know what you mean,' he said. 'I used to think exactly the same thing. But in reality so many species are in danger of extinction that we're actually helping to keep them alive with our breeding programmes in zoos. Do you remember the tapirs from earlier?'

'Yes.'

'Well, there are only about three thousand Malayan tapirs left in the wild. In around twenty to thirty years they'll probably be extinct.'

'That's really sad,' said Cora.

'Our research done while breeding them here also helps them in the wild,' added Eoin, 'because the information helps scientists figure out ways to help them survive.'

'And another thing,' Andy continued. 'It gives ordinary people the opportunity to see animals that they wouldn't otherwise see. And, even more importantly, it gives us the chance to educate people about the plight of these beautiful animals.'

Cora nodded slowly.

He looked at her gravely. 'It's far from ideal, but it's the best we can do just now,' he finished.

Cora had to admit that she was surprised by Andy's explanation. Both boys obviously cared deeply for these animals. She had not expected to find compassion on this planet. Maybe things weren't so black and white. Maybe there was a spectrum. Maybe things weren't always what they seemed. Maybe not all Earthlings were selfish murderers.

It was a lot of maybes. She'd need to think about them.

The children chatted for a long time as they wandered around the zoo looking at the different animals. Cora was really charmed by the animals – she saw a number of species they didn't have on SLOI.

Eoin could see that Cora was enchanted with the animals. 'You haven't been here before, have you?' he asked. He thought it was very strange that anyone could never have been to a zoo. He wondered where on Earth this girl came from. 'Do you live far away?'

'I'm from a long way away,' Cora said quietly. She didn't meet his eye.

'What are you doing here by yourself then?'

'Oh, it's a long story.' Her reply was purposely vague.

'So where are you staying?' asked Andy.

'Um, I hadn't really figured that out just yet,' she admitted. She couldn't say that she had thought about returning to the safety of the space capsule when the sunlight moved to the other side of the globe.

'Don't you have friends or relatives you can stay with?' said Eoin.

He tilted his head slightly and studied her for a moment through narrowed eyes, wondering if she had run away from home. One thing was for sure though, this girl needed a safe place to stay. 'Look, Cora, it's not really wise for anyone to be out wandering around on their own at night. Shall I ask Mum if you can stay at ours?'

'Oh, no. No. It's okay, thanks,' she quickly protested. 'I really don't want to be any trouble. I'll find somewhere.' She was worried that an adult might be more inclined to notice that she was different. And she didn't like the adults on this planet anyway.

Eoin nodded. 'Anyhow,' he continued, 'I heard Aunty Jas asking if Chloe and Skip could stay the night cos she has to go into work early in the morning.'

Deep in thought, Eoin made a steeple of his fingers and held them to the point of his nose. 'How about the tree house?' he said excitedly to his brother. As he spoke he dropped his hands away from his face and raised a palm upwards, as if he was stretching out food to one of his beloved animals. He turned to Cora. 'Why don't you stay in our tree house? It's in the woods at the back of the zoo, near where we live. You'd be safe there. It has camp beds so you and Loopy would be comfortable.'

Cora pondered for a moment before deciding that having more time to spend with these Earthlings might be useful. She knew she'd be safe enough with Loopy around.

'Sure. I would be happy to take up your offer, if that's okay,' she said, though she was wondering how a tree could also be a house.

'That's settled then, let's go,' he said, planning to have a chat with his mum when he got home.

It turned out that the tree house was a wooden structure *attached* to a tree. A huge tree. The tree trunk was so wide that Cora thought it might take all three of them joining hands to stretch the whole way around. There were six slotted steps up to the wooden door. The construction was set high off the ground, lodged firmly between thick, supporting branches. It had once been blue – quite a few years ago by the look of the cracked and peeling paint. The delicious woodsy smell of damp earth and greenery was wrapped around it like a protective cloak.

As the children climbed the steps Eoin turned to ask Cora if she would need help with Loopy but the collie was already bounding up behind them. 'I know collies can jump but I've never seen one jump like that before,' he said laughing. 'Has she got springs on her feet or something?'

Four grubby red beanbags were scattered on the floor and two camp beds were stacked in a corner. They were partly covered by a messy assortment of coloured sleeping bags and pillows. The grimy windows were covered in spiderwebs. Bits of dead leaves and dried grass reordered themselves in the draught from the open door.

'Is that your house?' Cora asked, nodding towards a side window.

Eoin came to stand beside her. 'Sure is,' he said. 'And look at that view of the hills,' he continued, pointing through a slightly less grimy window at the front. 'You can even see some of the animal houses.'

'It is a beautiful setting,' Cora breathed.

A loud snapping noise caused heads and bodies to twist around. Loopy was standing in the corner chomping. A hairy yellow and green spider that had previously been sitting in a web seemed to have mysteriously disappeared. Loopy looked like she was grinning. Unlike some nitwit dogs, *she* never missed.

The boys each flopped onto a beanbag, long legs pointing out in front of them like arrows. Cora followed suit and Loopy curled up on the remaining one.

It had already been a very long day. The brothers had been working hard in the zoo and the travellers had come a very long way from another world.

Cora smiled at Loopy, who was so tired that she had even stopped thinking about food and quickly dozed off.

The children chatted for a while and Eoin finally asked the question Cora had been dreading.

'So, where exactly are you from?'

Cora had spent the last few hours observing these children very carefully. Her thoughts had battled long and hard. Could she call these children friends? How could she ever call them friends? They were Earthlings. They seemed nice, though. They genuinely cared about the animals. Eoin had even talked about wanting to be a pilot for an aid agency when he left school, delivering supplies to places where people were starving. Cora had struggled to keep quiet at that. Starving! That some people on this planet had no food was unimaginable. What kind of savages ruled this place? How could that be allowed to happen? But it showed that at least these boys were thoughtful and compassionate.

Something shifted in her mind.

She gave a long sigh.

That was when she made the decision that would change everything.

Friendship

Cora took a another deep breath.

'Okay. This is kind of difficult because it might sound a bit far-fetched,' she offered cautiously, smoothing her eyebrow. Once again she seemed to find it difficult to meet their eyes.

'That's okay,' encouraged Eoin. 'They say truth can be stranger than fiction.'

Cora carefully removed her invisible hat. 'Loopy.'

Loopy was instantly awake and alert.

'Can you make my hat visible, please?'

The boys' faces wore the same puzzled expression. What was she talking about? Why was she miming holding a hat? There was no hat. This made no sense. They glanced at each other, suddenly wary of this strange girl.

All of a sudden a black hat appeared in Cora's hands.

The boys had seen magic tricks before, so although they were a bit surprised, they weren't really that shocked.

'O-kaaay.' Eoin turned his palms upward. 'So you can do magic.'

'No,' said Cora. 'I'm from SLOI. Another planet.' The words tumbled out of Cora's mouth all in one breath, before she could change her mind.

Eoin and Andy exchanged another uneasy look.

'Stop that, Cora,' said Andy. 'Don't make things up. It's not funny.'

Cora sighed as Loopy made the hat invisible again. She held it out to Andy who reached out and cautiously touched it.

'I can feel the hat,' he said. 'I just can't see it.'

'Skorbot,' she said, rolling her eyes. They still didn't believe her. 'Loop, do something else.'

Cora's feet and Loopy's paws gently lifted off the floor as they rose towards the tree-house roof.

Andy's eyes almost popped out of his head and Eoin's jaw hit the ground like a bag of rusty spanners. If you'd looked closely, you could probably have seen his tonsils.

'Am I really seeing what I think I'm seeing?' Andy rubbed his eyes with his knuckles. He couldn't tear his gaze away from Cora and Loopy floating in the air, even to look at his brother.

'I hope so,' said Eoin, 'because I think I'm seeing it too.'

'Okay Loopy,' Cora said.

They gently returned to the floor.

Eoin and Andy were speechless.

Cora felt guilty that she could not explain her reason for being on Earth. However, something at the back of her mind was slowly shifting, bending.

Was the change dangerous?

Maybe.

'Uh, um, okay then,' said Andy, finding his voice. 'Tell us about this place where you're from.'

'Well it's a satellite planet. Kind of like what you would call a moon.'

The boys' eyes never left her face.

'It orbits a large planet light years from your solar system and is beautiful place. It has similarities to the planet you call

Jupiter, but in more colours and shades, and it has rings like the planet you call Saturn. The main ring is ultra magnetic and made up of energy particles that contain knowledge.'

'How can a planet's ring be made up of knowledge?' asked Eoin. 'Knowledge isn't something solid. That doesn't make any sense.'

'Before the time known as the *great technological advance* the name for the planet was Crintal but since the Super Loop came on-line most of us just refer to it as the the Super Loop Of Information. That's where the name SLOI comes from. It's an acronym. Loopy could explain it better because her collar has a WooFi chip that's linked in to the Super Loop Operating System, that's SLOS – it's how we access the knowledge in the ring.'

Two heads and four wide eyes turned to look at Loopy. Eoin shook his head. He was convinced his ears could not possibly be working properly.

'So Loopy has access through the link to all the knowledge and information of SLOI,' Cora continued.

Loopy was nodding her head.

A proverbial penny began to drop through Eoin's grey matter. 'What do you mean "Loopy could explain"?' he said.

'Oh yes. That's something else.' Cora paused. At the back of her mind she pushed through the hesitation in telling these boys everything. 'Loopy can talk,' she finally admitted. She watched them carefully, waiting for their response.

The brothers looked down at Loopy, then at each other, then at Loopy again.

'Hi,' said Loopy. She flashed her collie smile.

If the boys were flabbergasted before, now they were completely gobsmacked.

'Wh . . . Wha . . . Whuu?' said Andy.

'Oh, I am so happy to be able to talk again,' said Loopy. 'It's not easy being quiet all day, you know, but Emperor RAMcoat told me to be silent when there are humans around.'

Eoin jumped to his feet. 'At the zoo earlier – with the chimps – I could have sworn I heard you thank Loopy for the poop slinging. I thought I saw her nod at you. And I was sure I saw her smirk. I thought I was going crazy.'

Cora smiled. 'You were right. Loopy keeps me safe.'

'And your names . . . RAMcoat? ROMhat?' The computer nerd was almost beside himself. 'Random access memory, and read only memory! Your names are connected with computer memory?'

'Emperor RAMcoat can change his mind but has to stay on SLOI, near the data source, to retain his memory. My ROM is portable. I can't change what's stored in my memory but I can add new data. So I can travel further away from SLOI.'

'Wow,' whispered Eoin, aware that he was in the presence of a fundamentally earth-shattering revelation.

'My ROM is linked to SLOS through my hat, my *ROMhat*, and the Emperor's RAM is linked through his coat.'

'Awesome,' Andy whispered. Although he didn't fully grasp everything she was going on about, he knew it was something incredible.

'The commander of our space fleet is Commander Amander HardDrive. Her portable database is located in her spacecraft, so she can access SLOS from anywhere,' said Cora.

'Why did you come here rather than her then?' asked Eoin.

'Well, Loopy has WooFi in her collar and the Emperor reckoned I could blend in better with the locals. The Commander is quite a conspicuous character. Obstinate. Maybe even reckless.'

‘Like a storm trooper from *Star Wars*?’ asked Andy, still struggling with the concept.

‘Probably,’ said Cora, who really wasn’t sure what that was but was actually very pleased that the boys were so curious.

They stayed up talking for a long time, asking Cora many more questions. She had initially been worried about being handed over to the authorities but really all she saw was kindness and acceptance. It had given her a lot to think about. She was beginning to wonder if her decision on this planet’s destiny was really as straight-forward as she had thought.

‘One final thing,’ said Eoin. He noticed it was getting quite late and their dad would be coming to look for them soon – and *nobody* wants their dad coming to look for them. ‘What’s *skorbot*? I’ve heard you say it a few times.’

Cora looked at the ground. Her voice was quiet.‘It’s a place – *was* a place. A very evil place.’

‘Like hell?’ said Andy.

‘Worse. It was a planet. It was inhabited by a race of beings . . .’

She drew a deep breath, trying to compose herself.

‘It was robot technology at its worst. A species where humanoids had merged with technology. Awesomely terrifying.’

‘Wow, that sounds incredible. How was it bad?’ asked Eoin.

‘Although they were advanced they weren’t able to free themselves of cybernetics. They actually physically assimilated with their technology. The Sloians didn’t have to do that. We are smarter. We connect with technology through the links I mentioned earlier, like Loopy’s collar and my hat. Skorbots secretly came to our world and mingled with the population. We didn’t even notice at first . . . only when the children began to disappear. They were stealing them. Taking them to their own planet to assimilate them.'

'Why did they have to steal children?' asked Andy.

'They had no children of their own,' said Cora. 'Something to do with bio-genesis. The bionic technology gave them robotic limbs, electronic eyes and who knows what else, but they could no longer breed.'

Eoin took a deep breath. He suspected what was coming next but he had to ask. 'What happened?' he said quietly.

Cora pressed her lips tightly together as if she didn't want the words to come out. 'We had no choice. They had stolen children!'

The boys nodded, encouraging her words. They needed to know the truth.

'We had to destroy the planet.' She paused. 'Rumour has it that some of the Skorbots still live – ones that were on other planets. We can only hope that is not true. Goodness only knows how their vile technology would have evolved by now.'

'What about the SLOI children? Did you get them back?' asked Andy.

Cora looked at the floor again. She sadly shook her head. 'The Skorbots were an incredibly greedy race. When their plans to assimilate the children didn't work they sold them to passing traders as slaves.'

Eventually, when the boys had partially recovered from their shock, they left Cora and Loopy to settle down for the night, reassuring her that they would keep her secret. They were glad that the girl and her dog were safely off the streets. If they had known the full story they would have been less concerned about Cora's safety and more concerned about the Earth's safety.

But Cora felt as if the heavy weight she'd carried for the past three years had lifted slightly. Again, she had the sensation of something shifting inside her.

Changing.

Turning.

Loopy was peckish again. 'Any chance of something to eat?' she asked Cora.

Cora laughed. 'Come on, you. Let's find some food outside.'

They climbed down the steps and sat down among the crunchy leaves in the quiet woods. A light wind whispered through the trees. An earthy smell of night-time damp hung in the air. Cora wasn't anxious in the woods because Loopy was with her. She would keep her safe. Dogs are good at that.

During another snack of worms and grass, Cora noticed apples sprouting on a nearby tree.

'I think that's what the animals were eating earlier,' she said, more to herself than Loopy, who was busy munching grass.

She walked to the tree, reached up and picked two shiny apples. She gave one to Loopy. The firm texture and the wonderful aroma as she crunched her way through the succulent apple was a nice surprise.

Loopy wasn't so surprised.

After eating their fill, they clambered back into the tree house and were soon fast asleep, Cora on a camp bed and Loopy curled up on a beanbag.

They'd had a mixed bag of good and bad that day but it seemed to have ended well enough. Cora thought it was a good job that her uncle had given her three days to observe and decide on the Earth's fate. She was very confused.

She had been surprised at how kind and generous some of the Earthlings could be. But she also knew that they could be as hostile as the Skorbots. But she had no idea just how true that was. Not yet.

The Nappers

Cora's brow furrowed. Her eyes shot open, then narrowed. Her heart pounded like a meteorite storm. She wasn't sure why, but she had the distinct feeling that something was very, very wrong.

She glanced at Loopy's beanbag.

It was empty.

Loopy? Where was Loopy?

Her breath caught, clutched by the icy finger of fear in her throat.

'Skorbot! Calm down. Calm down, Cora.' She spoke aloud in an effort to reassure herself. 'She's probably just gone outside for food again.'

Cora launched herself off the camp bed. She grabbed her invisible hat and bounded to the door of the tree house. Leaping all six steps at once, she dropped quickly to the grass.

The early morning Irish mist spread through the woods like a giant cataract. Malevolent. She shivered slightly in the eerie stillness.

She frantically looked around. There was no sign of Loopy.

She pulled her hat further over her head – partly for warmth, partly for comfort. Just in case it would help.

It didn't.

She continued to scan the woods.

Nothing.

Cora felt her heart drop like a heavy stone through wool. 'Loopy, oh Loopy, where are you?' Her soft voice was almost pleading.

'Please, please be here somewhere! I can't see you, Loopy!' Her words were wrenched from her soul as a wave of nausea crashed deep into the pit of her stomach.

It was terrifyingly familiar.

It had been three years since she had felt this way – the awful day she'd lost her parents in that senseless explosion. She'd always wanted to destroy this hateful planet but her uncle had always told her she was too young to understand. And now! And now he had sent her to this very place!

What had these Earthlings done now?

She felt her eyes sting. She didn't like tears. They were a sign of weakness. She needed to be strong.

One fat hot tear betrayed her as it escaped down her cheek. Then another. And another.

She began to run, flicking the tears away with the back of her hand. She searched the foliage in a frenzied attempt to find her friend – her most faithful companion, the little one who put up with her grumpy moods, who always accepted her just as she was. Who never judged her.

'No, no,' she cried, as more sobs dragged themselves through the air. 'I can't lose you as well – I just couldn't bear it. Oh, Loopy, Loopy, where *are* you? Why don't you answer me? I can't hear you, Loopy.'

She couldn't understand why Loopy wouldn't answer her. Loopy had been with her for ten years. She would never just ignore her.

An unspeakable explanation clawed its way through her mind.

She tried to push it back, but it persisted.

Loopy had been abducted.

But how? With Loopy's powers, how could that be possible? And who would have done such a thing? Who would steal an ordinary collie dog? Could it have been those horrid girls who attacked her the day before? No-one could know Loopy's secret. The only people who knew the truth about Loopy were the Ryan brothers. But weren't they her friends?

Her heart broke to think that they might have betrayed her, but really, what else could she expect from Earthlings?

They had already murdered her parents.

Suddenly something flashed in the monotonous mist.

Iridor.

Cora stumbled towards it in a trance. Roots and foliage grabbed at her feet as if trying to hold her back. She swept down and, as she scooped it up, her eyes focused more clearly.

She cried out in despair.

It was Loopy's collar.

Gripping it tightly in both hands she held it close to her chest. She turned her face to the clammy grey sky. 'I make this solemn oath,' she said quietly. Her voice was tight, constricted with pain. 'If you harm her . . .' Her voice surged into a scream of fury. 'I WILL DESTROY THIS PLANET!'

Then, in a tsunami of grief, she crumpled to the ground.

'You really are an old silly, y'know. You can't climb a tree – you're a dog. Dogs don't climb trees, Sniffy.'

A far-away voice wafted through the still morning air, pinging its way through to Cora's mind.

It was Chloe.

Talking to Skippy.

A dog.

A dog could pick up a scent.

A dog could help her find Loopy!

'Chloe. CHLOE!' Cora yelled, regaining her voice. 'Please help me!'

She pushed herself up from the undergrowth, still clutching Loopy's WooFi collar.

Chloe appeared out of the mist with Skippy lolloping at her side. 'Cora, what's happened?' she said.

She stared at the scratches, streaks of mud and decomposing leaves on Cora's filthy knees and hands. Cora's tear-streaked face and red eyes warned her that it was something really bad.

'Loopy has disappeared! I can't find her,' cried Cora, holding up the collar. 'I just don't know what to do.'

Two heartbeats passed as Chloe stared at the collar. She recognised it straight away. She never could make up her mind what actual colour it was.

Then she snapped into action. 'Okay. Let Skippy sniff the collar and pick up her scent,' she said. 'The boys are just back there. I'll get them and we'll all help you look. Now GO!' she shouted and scampered off towards the clearing where the Ryan brothers were throwing a rugby ball. 'Eoin! Andy!' she bellowed.

Cora's hands were shaking as she held the collar out for Skippy to sniff. She gently stroked the dog's teddy-bear head. Tears were streaming down her face, betraying her once more.

'Skippy, can you find Loopy? Find Loopy? Please,' she begged in a panic-filled voice.

A pair of brown eyes looked up at Cora. Skippy turned towards the collar. Her nose wrinkled as she sniffed, almost in distaste. Picking up the scent, she realised who the collar belonged to. They wanted her to find that Princess Lucinda thingy collie. Was she lost? Huh. Skippy didn't get lost. She was too smart. She always stayed near the pack.

Skippy began to sniff at the ground, her head moving back and forth over the damp earth as she snuffled through the undergrowth. Her tail whipped through the air like a broom flicking across a kitchen floor. She was always keen to please, and she liked Cora. She'd find that collie princess for her.

Swiftly she picked up a trail. She looked around to check that she had Cora's full attention, then she began to move forward, her nose sniffing and snuffling along the ground.

Cora followed, wringing Loopy's collar in her hands. They seemed to be headed toward the grounds of the zoo.

All of a sudden heavy thuds thundered through crackling foliage. Footsteps. People were calling her name. It sounded like Andy.

She swung round and shouted back, 'I'm here. Over here!'

Out of the mist darted Eoin and Andy, with Chloe doing her best to keep up.

'What happened?' asked Eoin, arriving first. Leaning over, he rested his hands on his knees as he tried to catch his breath.

'I don't know,' said Cora. 'Loopy just disappeared. I found her collar but I can't find her anywhere. I think Skippy has picked up her scent.'

'Someone must have taken her,' said Andy, hot on Eoin's heels. 'But why wouldn't she just float away?'

Chloe caught up. She looked puzzled. 'Float?' she echoed, almost hyperventilating. She could run really well but those boys could go like nuclear missiles.

'They've taken off her WooFi collar,' answered Cora 'and she couldn't even call out to me if Earthlings took her.' Her head dropped and silent tears began yet another journey over her now blotchy skin.

'Call out?' echoed Chloe, in confusion. When no one answered her, she decided that Cora, in her despair, had completely lost the plot.

'Okay, then, come on. Let's get moving. We'll find her,' said Eoin. He touched Cora gently on the shoulder. 'I promise.'

Skippy had picked up a clear trail, leading the children towards the grounds of the zoo, as Cora had suspected. The back gate, which was always kept locked, was wide open. The boys quickly tried to pull it closed and secure it as best they could while the girls continued to dash after Skippy. They followed her a long way – past the wild animal enclosures and right through the zoo. The boys quickly caught up – thankfully most of the route was downhill.

'Where are you even *taking* us, Sniffy?' panted Chloe, whose eight-year-old legs were working very hard to keep up with four furry legs, two rugby players and an incensed alien.

'I think we're headed towards the farm animals,' shouted Eoin. 'Andy, what's down there that would be useful to a dognapper?'

'Nothing really.' Andy was moving as fast as he could. 'There isn't anywhere to hide anything . . .' His voice dragged off as he kept thinking. 'Unless . . . Maybe the grain store – where they keep the farm animals' food? It only gets opened in the afternoons for the children to feed them. That's quiet, all right. And it's not on the main visitors' route either.'

'Looks like you were right.' Eoin dropped his voice as Skippy skidded to a halt at the dark green building. It had smooth metal walls and a black corrugated roof, but no windows. The sliding door along one side was very slightly open.

The children slid up to Skippy and listened outside the door, placing their ears as near as they dared.

Two men were arguing inside.

'I thought you said this mutt could talk,' one man shouted at the other.

'It can. I tell you, I've heard it!'

'Rubbish! It hasn't said a word since we nabbed it and it's not much use in a circus if it doesn't actually do anything, now is it? I'm hardly going to give you any money for that!'

'Well,' snarled the second man, 'what do you expect? If I shot you with a tranquilizer dart I don't think you'd have too much to say for yerself, would you?'

'If it's able, I'll find a way to make it talk. I can think of a few things,' he sneered menacingly.

'Aye, and if that doesn't work then we'll just get rid of the skanky mutt,' said his accomplice. 'Come on. We need to get out of here or we'll miss the boat.'

His voice trailed off as he gave a loud, rattling sniff as mucous slithered up his nose and into his throat.

Eoin's jaw dropped. 'It's Rob Snufflebot,' he whispered, wide-eyed.

'The other one sounds like Percy Piddler, the animal trainer from the circus,' said Chloe, who'd recently been there with her mum.

'Right, let's get this useless mutt into the van,' they heard Piddler order. 'You shouldn't have thrown away its collar. We might have got a few bob for that. It looked good quality.'

'It was only an ole collar. Would just have got in the way,' said Snufflebot, sounding even more shifty than usual, if that was possible.

'We need to move fast. Does anybody have a plan?' whispered Eoin urgently.

'I DO!' thundered Cora, now incandescent with rage.

Four heads spun towards her.

Before they could stop her, Cora delivered a well-placed gravity-boot kick to the edge of the door. It shot fully open. At the same time she wrenched her invisible hat over her face and shrieked with the ferocity of a mutant banshee.

The startled dognappers were taken unawares as the screaming, headless body blasted through the door. It staggered towards them as they turned to see some sort of deranged kamikaze warrior with outstretched arms, whose only intention was to slaughter them all in its deathly grip.

Rob Snufflebot was halfway through the exit to where a white van was waiting. The words *Rogue Brothers Circus* were painted on it in black lettering. The doors were open and the engine was already running while they had been loading it with sacks of animal feed.

'Aaaaaah! What *is* that?' Percy shrieked. The sack in his arms wriggled like an electric eel.

'Just get out – NOW! Before it kills us both!' Snufflebot yelled. 'I told you it was a stupid idea to stop for the grain.'

Skippy bounded in with bared teeth, snarling and barking furiously.

The other children rushed through the door after her – but it was too late.

Piddler flung the sack into the van, before leaping in after it. At the same time, Snufflebot jumped into the driver's seat, and the van sped off.

Cora pulled the hat back up so she could see again just as Chloe ran into the grain store behind the boys.

'No!' she cried.

The children looked at each other.

'Think, think, THINK,' Eoin urged himself. He held his head in his hands, long legs marching up and down.

Suddenly he stopped dead. He flung his arms wide. 'Okay. Okay. I've got it. Quick, follow me,' he ordered, galloping towards a large green shed.

Andy looked puzzled. 'Eoin, what –'

'Lawnmower!' screamed Eoin.

They stared at him. He had obviously gone mad.

Follow Your Nose

Outlines and shapes from the rest of the world began to materialise through the early morning mist as the circus van maneuvered its way towards the main gate of the zoo. An open gate was ready for the daily food deliveries from the market.

The quiet was shattered as an ear-splitting rumble burst from the garden-equipment shed. An enormous red ride-on lawnmower roared its way through the double doors.

Eoin sat behind the steering wheel, the other children perched and clung somewhat precariously to the inside of a large metal trailer attached to the back as it bumped its way towards the gate.

Skippy ran alongside, barking and leaping round in circles. Her mouth was open wide and her pink tongue hung over her teeth on one side. She was having a lot of fun.

Eoin had to yell as Skippy was making so much noise. 'I've switched off the mower bit so we can drive on the road. Which way did they go?'

Andy stood up and pointed. 'I can see them over there,' he shouted.

'You're behind me, Andy. I can't actually see where you're pointing,' complained Eoin.

'Sorry. Sorry. Just keep going straight ahead.'

'Slippy, be quiet, and follow Loopy in the van,' ordered Chloe.

Skippy's head twisted to glance at Chloe. Skippy was already having a very strange day. She kept thinking she could hear words inside her head – words like, 'This way, nitwit.' And now Chloe was telling her to follow a van. She usually got told off for chasing things. But she was also delighted. They'd clearly put her in charge of the pack. They'd finally figured out how clever she was.

She came. She barked. She conquered.

She darted in front of the mower and began to run faster, following the direction of the words in her head. They seemed to be coming from the van in front.

'I think Skippy's got the scent again,' said Chloe.

She turned towards Cora, noticing that she had become very quiet. She gently took her hand. 'Don't worry, Cora,' she said, 'we won't let anything happen to Loopy. I haven't a clue what's going on here, but we'll get her back.'

'Thank you,' said Cora, as her eyes filled with tears again. She was overwhelmed by the kindness of her new friends. How could she ever have thought they had anything to do with taking Loopy?

The van moved faster than the mower, and was quickly out of sight, but Skippy continued to run on in front, following the strange voice in her head.

'Where do you think we're headed?' Andy called out to his brother.

'Looks like it's towards the docks,' shouted Eoin over his shoulder.

'Yeah, they mentioned a boat. That sounds about right.'

As they followed Skippy, the gigantic bright yellow structures of the Harland and Wolff shipyard cranes began to grow larger on the horizon, towering high above the Belfast skyline. Eoin now knew for sure where they were going as he steered the mower towards the docks.

'There! Over there!' yelled Cora. She pointed towards where the Rogue Brothers' van sat alongside a small, battered cargo ferry. *Seascape Ferries* was painted on the side.

An ominous silence enveloped the scene.

'It looks like the ferry's already loaded. It's ready to sail!' shouted Andy.

The children and Skippy leaped off the mower as if it was on fire. They bounded towards the cargo ramp. Percy Piddler was on the deck. He was wrestling frantically with a sack full of wriggling collie.

'Loopy!' Cora screamed, feet pounding onto the ferry.

Andy stopped dead. He plucked his trusty catapult from its usual place in his back pocket. He didn't carry ammunition as a rule but he rummaged in another pocket and found an walnut. He placed the walnut in the catapult and sent it whizzing through the air like a heat-seeking missile – straight towards Piddler.

Eoin was right. His brother really did have a keen eye.

The walnut connected with a loud snap on the side of Piddler's head. Catching him by surprise, it knocked him off balance.

Then the sack swayed to the side, causing Piddler to overbalance even further.

Both Piddler and the sack landed in a heap on the deck.

Andy and Cora dived towards the wriggling sack.

Andy Ryan, the only boy to have ever actually used a Swiss Army knife to take a stone out of a horse's hoof, used it to quickly cut through the knot on the sack.

Out popped a little wet nose. Then a furry face. Loopy wriggled her way out of the sack. She shook herself free, head to tail.

'It's about time,' she grumbled.

Chloe's head swung towards Loopy. 'Did you . . . ? D-did Loopy really just speak?' she shrieked.

'Well, yes, of course. I'm safe now. Ooh, what's that . . .'

Loopy snapped up the walnut that had hit Piddler on the side of the head. It was a bit dented but she didn't really care. She hoped his head was also a bit dented.

Chloe giggled in delight. 'Awesome,' she said.

Cora dropped to her knees. A huge sob heaved its way up from the depths of her soul, shaking its way through her body. She hurled her arms around Loopy's neck and hugged the collie in a squeeze as tight as a pair of trousers after an emperor's feast.

'Oh, Loopy, I thought I'd lost you forever,' she cried. She nuzzled her head into the side of Loopy's neck. She inhaled the warm smell of the collie's fur, delighting in the softness against her face. At that moment nothing else in the world mattered. She gently slipped the WooFi collar back over Loopy's head.

'How did they get this off you, Loopy?' she said.

'I was drowsy. I heard rustling outside and thought it was a flock of starlings flapping about and went to investigate the noise.' Loopy lowered her eyes in embarrassment. 'Then they fired a tranquilizer dart from up in a tree.'

Meanwhile, Eoin had leaped towards Piddler, caught him in a rugby tackle, and pinned him to the ground. He quickly put his foot on the circus trainer's stomach. 'You're going nowhere, mate,' he growled. His eyes glowed like charcoal as he scowled at Piddler. 'Animals are not just things to be bought and sold,' he told him, through gritted teeth.

In the commotion, no-one noticed as a hatch on the deck slid open just a crack. One beady eye peered out. The hatch creaked once as it slowly opened wider. A dark figure wormed quietly out. Slinking silently as he skimmed along the deck, Snufflebot unfastened a hunting knife from the sheath on his right ankle. Leaping up to catch Eoin off guard, he slammed into his back. He thrust his left arm around Eoin's upper arms and, holding him in a vice-like grip, he pressed the knife against Eoin's throat.

'Hand over that scrawny mutt or this interfering bag of bones gets it,' Snufflebot snarled.

Andy's face paled as he turned to see his brother in the grasp of their revolting former assistant.

Seizing the opportunity, Piddler rolled and twisted on the ground, using his legs to push upwards and out from under Eoin's restraining foot.

Andy took a step towards them.

'Don't come any closer,' shouted Snufflebot. 'You interfering know-it-alls should have left us well alone. This is all your fault.'

'You self-centred evil ole git! Don't you dare blame us for your disgusting behaviour!' yelled Andy.

A voice screamed in Skippy's head. 'Don't just stand there, nitwit, *GET HIM*!'

Quick as a flash, with the precision of a homicidal ballerina, Skippy leaped on Snufflebot. She bit him on the wrist as her weight knocked him off balance. Skippy noticed that his wrist was very hard and her teeth didn't even seem to make much of an injury, but the knife still spun out of his hand as he landed with a powerful thud.

At the same time, Piddler dived towards Loopy, knocking her sideways on the deck.

'No!' screamed Cora, lurching towards Piddler. But he was bigger and faster. He shoved Cora hard on one side and she landed with thump on the deck.

Piddler's previous experience of Loopy was when she partially tranquilized and wriggling in a sack. So he was not prepared for the projectile speed of a ten-year-old canine alien missile. Loopy swished round and round, freeing herself from his vile grasp and, in the process, propelled him towards the guard rail. Now completely off balance, her momentum sent him on a wobbly dive overboard, straight into the ice-cold Irish Sea.

Finding her feet, Cora ran to the rail and peered over. Bubbles and arms flailed on the surface of the water.

For a second Piddler's head appeared. 'Help, I can't swim!' he gurgled.

'You really should have learned then,' said Cora, eyes flashing. She turned her back and walked away.

All of a sudden a loud explosion rocked the ferry.

All heads whipped round to see Chloe standing with the ferry's emergency flare gun aimed into the sky.

'Chloe, wh–' yelled Eoin.

The clatter of an outboard motor approaching at an incredibly fast speed drowned him out. Chloe silently raised her arm and pointed to the approaching boat. It was the harbour police.

'Help?' she said, turning her free hand upwards.

Skippy scrambled off Snufflebot as Eoin and Andy dragged him to his feet. She continued to snarl and bare her teeth, watching him intently. There was something very unsavoury about that man.

'What happened to Piddler?' Eoin called out to Cora.

'I think he jumped overboard,' she said casually.

Eoin ran to the rail. 'Did he get away?'

Cora shrugged, ignoring Loopy's reproachful look.

Eoin watched the harbour police speedboat slow down so that

two police officers could fish a bedraggled Piddler out of the water. He was coughing and spluttering, gasping loudly, trying to catch his breath, and honking like the ferry's fog horn. Snot, a couple of small crabs, bits of seaweed, and what looked like half the Irish Sea poured out of every orifice.

'What are we gonna do with this scumbag?' growled Andy. His heart pounded. His mouth was set in a firm line as his dark eyes burrowed into Snufflebot. Gripping the man's shirt collar, he twisted it tighter in his white knuckles. He wasn't about to let this scoundrel get away.

Cora marched up to Snufflebot. Ignoring the offensive smell, she stepped right in front of him. Orange-frizzy-blonde and Nose-ring Girl would have been proud.

She looked him in the eye. 'YOU are nothing more than a disgusting scab on this planet,' she said. 'If you are ever stupid enough to cross my path again, I will make sure you disappear. For good. Do you hear me?'

Two rheumy eyes flashed Cora a final look of contempt before lowering their gaze. He nodded.

As the ferry horn gave two final blasts for its impending departure and the harbour police hauled their slimy catch in for questioning, four exhilarated children and two happy dogs bounded over the cargo ramp towards dry land.

Skippy and Loopy were still alert – four ears up, sharp teeth bared, both ready for action if required. They were part of a new pack now.

'Let's get out of here,' Loopy said to the children, as soon they'd finished telling the police what had happened, and Snufflebot was handcuffed. 'And you too, nitwit,' she added, grinning at Skippy.

Skippy gave her a menacing look. 'Grrrrrr,' she said.

It looked like the crisis was over.
But then again, looks can be deceiving.

Danger! Sharp Bends Ahead

The pack arrived back at the zoo, just managing to return the mower to the shed before the zoo was opened to the public.

'Why don't you have breakfast with us, Cora?' said Andy, as they trudged towards the Ryan house.

Cora realised she was actually feeling quite hungry after the morning's adventure. It was a good bet that Loopy was also hungry – Loopy was always hungry.

'That would be great,' said Cora. She stroked Loopy's furry head again as they steered towards a nearby patch of grass.

'No, Cora, this way,' said a mystified Chloe.

The grey stone house where the Ryans lived reminded Cora a little of Mr Norman's castle, although it was not as dull. Its green-tiled roof blended with the peaceful surroundings. Either side of the white arched entrance door were two large windows. Higher up the building were three slightly smaller windows – Cora thought that some of the people who lived inside must be *really* tall to be able to see out of those.

Chloe led the way through the front door, and children and dogs followed her over a honey-coloured polished floor through a cream-painted hallway. Brightly coloured paintings adorned the walls. Their slightly lopsided scenery and matchstick people looked like they had been painted by children. Cora thought it was quite charming.

As Chloe opened the kitchen door, a mouth-watering aroma wafted though the air.

A dark-haired lady stood with her back to the door, stirring a pot on the cooker. 'I was just going to come to look for you lot,' she called over her shoulder. 'Breakfast is ready. You've just missed your dad. He's gone to work.'

'Mum, these are our friends, Cora and Loopy,' said Andy. 'Is it okay if they join us?'

Mrs Ryan turned to Cora with a welcoming smile. 'Of course it is,' she said. 'There's always plenty here for everyone.'

She fetched another plate from the cupboard and placed it on the table.

'It's lovely to meet you, Cora and Loopy,' said Mrs Ryan. She reached down and patted Loopy's head.

Loopy was sniffing the air. She quickly scanned the room, then she turned to give Mrs Ryan the hopeful-hungry-collie look. Loopy was obviously very relaxed here. That told Cora all she needed to know.

Cora liked Mrs Ryan immediately. She had a warm smile. Strangely, something about her reminded Cora of the Commander. Well, if the Commander had been given a sedative, maybe.

The children sat at an enormous wooden table that was covered with so much stuff you could hardly see the surface. Eoin explained it all to Cora – there were bowls of delicious chopped fruit and many different kinds of yoghurt. There were plates of fluffy scrambled eggs, potato bread, soda bread, pancakes, grilled mushrooms, tomatoes, and a huge plate of crusty toast. Cora had neither seen nor tasted anything like this before in her life. She was surprised at the selection of food. There were so many colours and textures that she had to try everything. She had never had such a delicious meal in all her life. Who would have believed that the Earthlings could actually do something better than the Sloians!

Mrs Ryan also made up two bowls filled with a selection of all the goodies for the dogs. Skippy was quite partial to an Irish breakfast, even though this one was vegetarian. Loopy was partial to anything that was edible, and actually quite a few things that weren't.

When breakfast was over, the children cleared up and washed the dishes while Mrs Ryan got ready for work but they didn't mention their morning adventure in case their mum asked too many questions about how they had met Cora.

The dogs were sent out the back to do what Skippy thought of as the *special stuff*. She knew it was special as it was obviously very important. Precious, even. Every time she did some, someone followed behind and picked it up in a pretty coloured bag. The bag was then tied in a knot and stored inside a special plastic bin on wheels.

She knew that once a week an enormous metal monster came growling, roaring, and screeching to the house. He moved backwards on enormous wheels and had a huge mouth with massive teeth. His name was Dennis because he had it written on his head in giant silver letters. She supposed it was in case he forgot who he was. Obviously he wasn't as smart as she was. Dennis's two assistants had to put the container with wheels on his bottom lip so he could tilt it backwards to swallow the contents. Then he mashed it all up with his enormous teeth.

Somewhere in her mind she heard the word 'nitwit'. She turned and saw Loopy looking at her. She noticed that Loopy did different special stuff. It had little shiny coloured bits of paper and foil in it. Loopy really was very odd.

When Mrs Ryan left for her job at the bank, the children continued to chat. Cora explained to Chloe about SLOI and SLOS. Chloe took it all in her stride. After all, she'd just heard a dog speaking.

Then Chloe asked a difficult question.

'Cora, of all the places you could have gone, why did you come to this planet?'

Cora now considered these children to be her friends. They had helped her through some of the worst hours of her life. She owed them the truth.

'I was sent here by my uncle,' she said.

'Your uncle?' the brothers chorused.

'Emperor RAMcoat is my uncle,' she said quietly. She smoothed her left eyebrow. 'He sent me here because my parents were killed . . . in an explosion . . . three years ago.' She lowered her eyes to stare at the floor.

There was complete silence in the room.

'A satellite crashed into an asteroid . . . The asteroid moved off course, smashed into my parents' space capsule . . . and . . . they . . . died . . .' Cora's voice trailed off.

'Oh no. How really, really awful,' breathed Andy. 'I'm so sorry.'

Another shocked silence followed while each child thought about how unspeakable it would be to lose their parents.

After a few moments, Eoin cautiously said, 'Cora . . . if you don't mind me asking . . . Um . . . What's the connection with Earth?'

As she absentmindedly stroked Skippy's head, Cora took a deep breath and exhaled through her mouth. Slowly she raised her head to look Eoin in the eye. 'It was a satellite from Earth. And it was made to crash into that asteroid on purpose.'

She swallowed the prickly lump in her throat and blinked away tears. 'The human race is selfish and careless. They do what they want with no thought for the consequences. Your people killed my parents.'

Eoin wasn't sure how to respond. He hesitated, then he spoke quietly. 'I remember reading about that. This planet is hit by asteroids on quite a regular basis.' He watched Cora carefully before deciding to continue. 'Small ones, that is. A large asteroid would wipe out our entire population.' His voice faltered, became barely a whisper. 'That's why they made the satellite crash. To knock the asteroid off course from Earth.'

Cora looked at him dumbly. Numb. 'To save your planet?' she whispered. Her eyebrows were raised. Her eyes were wide. The words crackled along her throat.

He nodded, not trusting himself to speak, and not really sure what else to say.

Andy leaned forward. Gentle fingers that had comforted many sick animals touched Cora's arm. 'I remember it too, Cora. We're honestly not making excuses,' he said softly, 'but it's important that you know it wasn't done to harm anyone else. We were never even really sure if there was other life out there.'

Silent tears slid down Cora's face. She barely noticed.

'For three years I've thought you murdered my parents,' she said in disbelief.

Chloe made no sound as big, fat tears burst out of her eyes and rolled down her little face. She reached out and took Cora's hand for the second time that day.

Cora's breath broke, and with a heaving wail she hugged the little girl.

'It's okay, Cora,' said Chloe. 'You've got us now. We're your new family.'

When lunchtime came, the children spread creamy butter, cheese, juicy tomatoes and lettuce on thickly cut bread. Cora thought it was wonderful. She decided there and then that she never wanted to eat worms and grass again. The children also shared their sandwiches with their canine friends. Loopy was delighted. She almost decided never to eat worms and grass again. Well, for maybe around one second.

In the afternoon the boys were due back at the zoo and Chloe volunteered to help them. Cora told them that she needed some time to prepare her report for Emperor RAMcoat and asked if she could go back to the tree house where she would not be in anyone's way. They weren't exactly sure what she was reporting on but left her to it as they set off to the zoo. They left Skippy in her care and Cora wondered if it was to ensure that she would be there when they returned.

Skippy decided she must be going insane. She'd spent most of the morning hearing that Princess Lucinda's voice *inside* her head and now she was hearing it *outside* her head. She decided to stop thinking about it because trying to figure it all out was giving her a headache. She followed Cora into the tree house, lay down, grumbled and went to sleep.

Cora thought quietly for a long time.

'Okay, Loopy,' she said,eventually, 'I think I've got it all straight in my head now. I'm ready to make my report.'

'You've still got another day.'

'I don't need that long, Loop.'

'Just take one more day. Just to be sure.'

'I don't think I'll change my mind, Loopy.'

'It's a very important decision, Cora. You need to be certain, that's all.'

'Okay, Loopy. So I will.' Cora laughed. 'Listen to me sounding all Irish.'

When the children returned from the zoo, their first stop was the tree house. Skippy was happy to see Chloe and did a bit of yowling, murff-murffing and whining.

'Anyone would think she was trying to talk,' said Chloe, laughing. 'Maybe Loopy could teach her.'

It was the one time that both dogs had the same thought: *not likely*!

A car horn beeped in the driveway. 'That's mum,' said Chloe. 'See you later.' She bounded down the tree house steps closely followed by Skippy.

'Mum said you've to come in for dinner,' Andy told Cora. 'We're having pizza.'

Cora smiled. 'Thank you,' she said, 'that would be lovely. We've never had pizza before.'

'Oh, you so need to prepare yourself to be amazed,' said Andy.

They ate together again at the big table in the kitchen. The pizza was one of Mrs Ryan's specialities and was covered in many different types of vegetables, an array of vibrant colours. Andy had not been exaggerating.

This time Mr Ryan was there and he had the same kind eyes and smiling welcome as his wife. And Cora could see where Eoin got his curly brown hair from.

'Well, it seems like you all had an interesting morning!' he said. The police had been in touch to tell him what the children had been up to and to let him know that they had Snufflebot and Piddler in custody. He told them about the mysterious break in at the zoo that morning and the missing tranquilizer dart gun. He also reported that they were fully staffed again as the ticket assistant who had been ill seemed to have made a speedy recovery.

'And how's Tina the tapir doing?' Mrs Ryan asked.

Andy told them that she seemed to be getting a little bit taller every day. She was a big hit with the visitors.

The children talked on about their day at the zoo. Cora was impressed that the parents actually sat down and took an interest in what the children had to say. They seemed to realise how important it was. It reminded Cora of when her parents were alive. It brought a warm feeling to her neck – just behind the ears. She recognised it: it was the bittersweet feeling of coming home.

They were almost finished eating when the doorbell rang. Mrs Ryan left the table to go and see who it was. They heard her surprised voice and laughter in the hallway. She returned a few minutes later accompanied by a man in a dark grey pinstripe suit.

'This is Mr Smiley. My boss from the bank. He's just come to tell me some news. It seems he's retiring at the end of the month,' she told the family.

'Please, call me Riley,' he said. They all smiled politely and shook his hand.

Cora decided that his name suited him as he was indeed very smiley, but Loopy surreptitiously sniffed the sleeve of Riley Smiley's coat. She wasn't so sure.

Eoin disappeared, and Cora and Andy went outside with the dogs, leaving the Ryan parents chatting to Riley Smiley.

'Where's Eoin gone?' Cora asked.

'Oh him. He's probably glued again. As usual,' said Andy, his features arranged in a scowl.

'Glued? Stuck to something?' asked Cora, somewhat puzzled. It was the best her lexicon could suggest.

Andy rolled his eyes. 'Aye. May as well be.'

She noticed his eyes seemed darker and he had a surly expression on his face.

'Glued to the computer, if y'must know,' he said. 'I think he sometimes forgets where the off switch is.'

Suddenly the door swung open and Riley Smiley strolled out. He lifted his arm and waved goodbye to everyone, including the children, then he got into his car. The somewhat smug smile remained on his face.

Cora noticed that, as soon as he got into the car, he began to type something into his mobile phone. She reckoned it must be something important if it needed to be done before he could even drive off.

'Anyway, shall we go to the shop?' said Andy. 'I've got some pocket money and I want to get some gobstoppers.'

Cora wondered what pocket money was. It must be the money they kept in their pocket. After all, Andy seemed to keep everything else he owned in his pockets.

'What's a gob? What do gobstoppers stop it from doing?'

'Just about everything.' Andy laughed. 'They're really hard sweets and they last for ages. They're massive so they fill your whole mouth – your gob. You can't even speak.'

Cora looked at Loopy. As expected, Loopy was standing to attention – ears alert, head tilted to one side, eyes as wide as saucers.

'I think that's a yes to us coming along,' she said.

It sounded interesting.

And it was.

And it was also one of a sequence of events with grave consequences.

For the friends. For the planet.

Sweet and Sour

The children strolled down the road towards the shop.

A sign on the glass doorway stated, ONLY HELPING DOGS ALLOWED.

'Allowed what?' Cora said.

'In,' said Andy. 'Only helping dogs are allowed in to the shop.'

'Then they haven't finished the sentence. Does anyone bother with grammar in this place?'

'Not much,' said Andy.

'Loopy's a helping dog, right?'

'Um, not according to the rest of the planet.'

Although Cora hated to be separated from Loopy, she was reassured when she went inside when she could see the curious furry face and wet nose poking round the door frame.

The sweetie smell was making Loopy's mouth water. There were many different shapes and sizes with lots of brightly coloured wrappers. She recognised a lot of the wrappers as ones she had chased along the road. She had noticed how it made her poop look interesting. Well, if you're interested in that sort of thing, that is. The other dog, Skippy, seemed to be. Loopy couldn't understand why anyone would be interested in poop but she had already decided that Skippy was a bit of a nitwit.

Unfortunately the sales assistant wasn't much interested in

the customers. She wore a bored expression as she put the money in the till and scooped out Andy's change.

However, as soon as her mobile phone buzzed she perked up. Still holding the change in her hand, she picked up the phone and studied a message. Eventually she remembered she was still holding Andy's change and carelessly flopped it into his hand.

Cora thought this was incredibly rude but Andy hardly appeared to notice. He was used to this type of behaviour.

When they left the shop, Andy had a bag full of gobstoppers. He took one out and held it up between his thumb and forefinger to allow Cora to inspect it. She peered at it – a swirly mixture of green, blue and pink that would fill a child's whole mouth.

Cora laughed. 'It looks like a small planet,' she said. 'I don't think I'll bother. It's huge! Thanks, anyway.'

'I think *I'll* bother,' said a voice somewhere in the region of her left knee.

The children gazed downward. Loopy's mouth opened to display four collie incisors behind a cheeky grin.

'Yes, please,' she said, turning up the collie smile to full volume.

Andy shook his head. He wondered if there was anything Loopy wouldn't eat. 'We really shouldn't give sweets to animals,' he said.

'Don't worry,' laughed Cora. 'I think Loopy's digestive system might be different from other animals on this planet.'

Andy leaned down and offered Loopy the gobstopper. She tried to chew it but all she could do was make noisy slurping noises.

'Uh oo ii ooo?' she gurgled.

'You can't chew it, Loopy,' said Andy. 'You just suck it and it will eventually dissolve.'

'Uh eh i ane eek.'

'It's all right, Loop. You don't need to speak. Is it nice?' said Cora.

Loopy nodded her head vigorously. 'Mmmmmmglu,' she said, as she experienced the smooth, sugary raspberry and lime flavour.

She quickly closed her mouth and began to trot along like a normal collie when a group of Earthlings appeared. She reckoned that the Snufflebot villain must have heard her speaking at the zoo. She vowed to herself that she would never let that happen again. Some of these Earthlings were downright evil. Yet some were also really nice. Like Andy. And Chloe. And Eoin. And their family. Anyone would think there were two types of humanoids on this planet.

Cora felt something jolt her left arm.

A girl had bumped into her whilst distractedly reading a message on her phone. She automatically adjusted direction without even glancing at Cora, let alone apologising.

'Seriously Andy! I still have problems with how humans treat each other sometimes,' she said. 'They are so wrapped up in themselves –'

'Aaaa eirr echnulugeee,' Loopy managed to gurgle.

Cora reckoned Loopy was saying something about technology, and gave her a nod.

'They don't even seem to notice other people,' continued Cora. 'They are just so unpleasant.'

'Yeah, that's when they even bother to leave the house,' he agreed. 'Our Eoin's getting worse. We can't seem to peel him away from his computer games at all these days. And if it's not that, then he's reading messages from his friends or playing games on *Livewire.* It really annoys me.'

Cora was about to reply when she was distracted by a shop called *Pat Butcher's.* A sign in the window advertised, LION STEAKS.

'Andy, please tell me that people don't eat lions,' she pleaded, appalled. She had seen the beautiful lions at the zoo.

'Oh. No,' he said. 'They mean *loin* steaks. It's a particular cut of meat from a pig. It's just spelled wrong, that's all.'

Cora's jaw dropped. She looked aghast. 'Skorbot. You eat snorklers?'

'Yeah, loads of people eat meat.'

Cora spun on her heel and marched towards the shop door. Loopy quickly followed, sniffing, thinking how interesting this all was.

The butcher was not happy.

'Oi! No dogs allowed. Get that thing out of here!' he demanded.

'You've got to be kidding me,' Cora said, eyes flashing.

'It can't come in. It's unhygienic,' the butcher snapped.

'Unhygienic?' screeched Cora. Speechless, she pointed to the window display. There was a fly. It wandered across a piece of what she could now identify as dead animal. She watched it stop to eat a minuscule piece of flesh. Obviously its stomach was unable to handle it and it vomited out what it had just eaten – back onto the meat. It then continued its journey onto the next piece of meat to establish if it could digest that any better. It couldn't.

Cora swung quickly towards Andy as he steered her back outside. 'This place is vile,' she said. 'Just remind me,' she thundered, 'why did I stay here another day?'

Andy shrugged his shoulders. 'Beats me. But when your ready

to go back to SLOI I'm coming with you,' he offered hopefully.

Cora looked at the ground to avoid eye contact. 'I'm not sure how that might work,' she said.

The children wandered back to the Ryan house. They found Mrs Ryan in the downstairs office, checking the mail on her computer.

Andy slowly shook his head. 'Aren't you supposed to be off work now, Mum?' he asked.

'Oh, yes dear,' she replied absentmindedly. 'I just need to check a couple of things and that's it.' She looked up and grimaced. 'I can't believe dear Mr Smiley is leaving at the end of the month. He says they're not paying him enough so he's going to take his pension and buy a house somewhere far away,' she chattered on.

'Where's Eoin, Mum?' Andy asked. He really wasn't bothered about Mr Smiley and his pension. He wasn't even sure if he liked the man. Too smiley. What was the old saying? Too sweet to be wholesome.

'I haven't seen him since dinner,' said Mrs Ryan. 'He must still be upstairs.'

Andy and Cora clumped up the stairs to look for his brother.

Cora smiled, somewhat embarrassed when she realised the reason for the windows higher up. The house had two levels. There were less people on SLOI so they didn't need to build upwards.

They found Eoin in the games room.

'I don't believe it,' said Andy. 'Eoin! Are you still on *Livewire*?'

'Mmm,' said Eoin distractedly, twisting the console controller quickly from side to side.

'You've been playing that game for hours. We've just made friends with real live aliens and your playing *Livewire*?' Andy could hardly believe it.

'Yeah, but my friends are on, so I can't just leave –'

He stopped speaking to shoot a zombie that had popped its head through a door – literally – it was holding its head in its left hand in an attempt to see round the corner.

Andy took a step forward and flipped off the screen.

'There you go,' he said. 'Consider yourself left.'

Eoin shot out of the chair and dived towards his brother. 'What do you think you're doing? I was playin' that!' he yelled right into Andy's face.

'Hey guys, calm down,' said Cora nervously. She could handle most situations but she really hated conflict. It was so unnecessary. 'Andy's just annoyed because you've been ignoring him a bit, Eoin, that's all.'

Eoin's eyes glinted as he shoved Andy hard on the shoulder. 'Don't EVER do that again.'

Andy bristled. He pushed back. 'And don't you EVER push me again or you'll be sorry.'

'Okay, guys. Seriously? If you two don't back off then we'll all be sorry. Calm down,' Cora added. She was getting worried. She hadn't seen Andy and Eoin angry with each other like this before. She realised it could easily escalate into an actual physical fight and was disappointed as it seemed that even nice Earthlings had rage simmering just below the surface, ready to explode.

Red-faced, Andy turned on his heel and marched out of the games room.

Cora looked at Eoin.

He shrugged.

She shook her head, sighing sadly. She thought so much of these boys even though she had only known them for two days. It made her very sad to see them angry with each other.

She decided that this must be something important. She knew that Earth had the internet, which was a basic version of SLOS, but she would have to investigate exactly what *Livewire* was.

She left Eoin in the games room and closed the door behind her. She could hear Andy talking to Mrs Ryan downstairs.

When she joined them in the office, Andy was complaining about the amount of time that Eoin spent on *Livewire*. Mrs Ryan listened patiently. She understood that Andy was frustrated as, until recently, the brothers had spent a lot of time playing rugby and exploring in the woods together.

'I know. I know, Andy. I hear what you're saying,' she said. 'But he is linked in to a game with his friends. What's so wrong with that? You were out with Cora, anyway.'

Andy shook his head in exasperation. No-one seemed to understand. He looked at Cora. She gave him a sympathetic half smile. He realised that someone did understand. She knew exactly what it was like to feel disconnected from family.

He stomped towards the front door. 'Well, if he'd rather be locked inside all day than live in the real world, see if I care,' he shot back over his shoulder.

Cora and Loopy quietly followed him outside.

'What exactly is this *Livewire* thing, anyway?' Cora asked, half running to keep up with Andy, who was crunching his way through the woods.

'It's a stupid social network site. It's supposed to link you up with friends and you can play games on it. It's all done through the internet. The kids in school talk about it constantly. Honestly, I'm sick of it. Technology is taking over this stupid planet. People don't even speak to each other properly any more.'

'Mmm, I noticed the girl in the shop and others in the street checking their phones, not even aware of what was going on around them,' said Cora.

'That's another thing,' ranted Andy, 'you ought to see how they text each other. They don't even bother with proper English. They abbreviate everything. I actually heard someone in school *saying* "LOL" as if it was a real word. They leave out letters and basically butcher the language.'

Cora shuddered. 'Don't talk to me about butchers,' she said. 'I've had enough dealings with butchers for one day, thank you very much.'

Andy laughed. Cora had diffused his anger.

For now.

What's Wrong with a Horse?

Following an attack of conscience, which would never be mentioned, Eoin had already joined his mum downstairs when Cora and Andy arrived back at the house. Chloe and her mother were also there.

Mrs Callaghan looked at Cora. 'Hello, Cora,' she said. 'I'm Jasmine. I've heard so much about you. Chloe hasn't stopped talking about you and your wonderful dog.' She laughed.

Cora gave her a shy smile.

Mrs Callaghan lowered her voice. 'She said that you had lost your parents. I'm so sorry to hear that.'

Warily, Cora nodded. 'Thank you.'

'Apparently you have an uncle? Is that who you live with?'

'Um, yes. I've been living with my uncle for three years. I'm just here for a visit.'

Cora hesitated, wondering exactly what Chloe had been saying and where this particular conversation was headed.

'So where is he then?' asked Mrs Callaghan.

Cora smoothed her eyebrow. 'Um. . . my uncle is in charge of a very large organisation so he works a lot.'

'So you're here in your own?' Mrs Callaghan exchanged a look with her sister as Cora nodded.

'Well, you'd be welcome to stay with us if you'd like. There's only Chloe and myself in the house –'

'And Skippy,' interrupted Chloe.

'Yes, and Skippy,' continued Mrs Callaghan. 'So we've plenty of room. I'd be happy to have a chat with your uncle to make arrangements. You could stay for as long as you like – if you wanted to, or needed to, that is . . .' she said, with a hesitant smile. 'It's not really safe to be out wandering around on your own'. She broached the subject as carefully as she could, worried that Cora might be a runaway.

Cora wondered if their kindness meant that things hadn't always been easy for this family either.

'We've been thinking of adding to our family,' Mrs Callaghan continued to chat, 'since Chloe's an only child.'

Cora was curious. How could Chloe be an only child? The planet was full of them.

'It would be lovely for Chloe to have a companion. She's actually been talking about another dog – or a horse!' Mrs Callaghan laughed.

'What's wrong with a horse?' said Chloe.

Everyone laughed – even Andy and Eoin, though they glanced uneasily at each other.

'Please say yes,' begged Chloe. 'I think Skippy really likes Loopy.'

Skippy wondered where Chloe had got that idea from. Then she figured out they probably just wanted another dog to collect even more special stuff to impress Dennis. She was doing her best, sometimes three times a day, but there's only so much one dog can do.

Cora's eyes misted slightly and, when she smiled, they almost made tears. 'That would be lovely,' she said. 'Thank you.'

Chloe flung herself towards Cora, wrapping her in a tight hug. Cora laughed and lifted the little girl off the ground, swinging her in a circle.

'Obviously I'll need to speak to your uncle,' said Mrs Callaghan, 'just to make sure it's okay for you to stay. Could I phone him now?'

Cora placed Chloe's feet gently on the ground as she tried to think quickly. 'Um . . .' she looked towards Eoin, wide-eyed.

'I know he has problems with his phone signal but I can help you with that,' said Eoin, grinning excitedly. He couldn't wait to see how Loopy communicated with SLOI through SLOS. And he was pretty sure they could get RAMcoat on a screen somewhere in the house. He decided that this situation was suddenly becoming more interesting.

'He'll likely be asleep just now,' said Cora.

'Oh right, that's fine. We can do it tomorrow then. That'll be grand,' said Mrs Callaghan. 'Okay, Chloe. Let's go and get the house ready for our visitor. Would you like to come with us now Cora or do you want to stay here for a while?'

'Andy and I were just chatting,' said Cora. 'Shall I come over in about half an hour?'

'Of course, you just come on over when you're ready Cora.'

Cora smiled to herself. Things seemed to be going well.

But she could not have been more wrong.

Mice and Ice

Andy and Cora took Loopy outside to play ball.

However, it turned out that Princess Lucinda believed that playing ball was beneath her. It was something that only nitwits did. Like You-know-who.

'If you want the ball then why do you keep throwing it away?' she asked Andy.

'You're supposed to fetch it,' Andy said.

'If you want it that much, go and get it yourself.'

Cora rolled her eyes.

They gave up and headed back to the house. Loud voices were coming from the living room.

'Uh, oh,' said Andy. 'You're in for a big treat – it's M'Granny.'

'What's M'Granny?' said Cora.

'It's not a "what" it's a "who",' said Andy, grinning like a maniac. 'Brace yourself.'

An elderly lady was perched regally on the sofa in the living room, alongside Mr Ryan. She blinked at them through round glasses so thick they could have been double glazed. One lens was much stronger than the other and it made that eye look frighteningly huge.

'Hi, Gran,' yelled Andy. 'This is my friend, Cora, and her dog, Loopy.'

'Loony? Who's a loony?' said M'Granny.

'Looo-*peee*,' emphasised Andy. 'She's deaf as a doorpost,' he whispered to Cora.

'Who peed?' she asked. 'It's those mice.' She waved a bony finger at Mr Ryan and shook her head. 'I told you.'

She turned to Cora. 'Is that dog any good at catching mice?' she asked, not bothering to wait for an answer. 'It's the mice *dirt*, y'see. It's everywhere. I'm tortured. He doesn't believe me.' She nodded her head towards Mr Ryan. 'They all think I'm bonkers. The mice run round the house all night, so they do. I hear them. They live in the bathroom where it's warm. They climb up the toilet roll and shred it all over the floor – every night, when I'm in bed. I find it in the mornings when I get up. And the *dirt*. Mice *dirt*. All over the bathmat. They love that bathmat,' she said, bobbing her head up and down like a plastic duck in water. 'I've tried rolling it up and hiding it on the shelf, but they still find it. And then there's mice *dirt* all over it. They love that mat,' she told Cora.

Cora had no idea how to respond, so she said nothing.

'Mum, it's not mice, it's only crumbs and dust.' Mr Ryan tried for the millionth time to explain.

'Mice *dirt*,' Granny replied. 'Nobody believes me.'

'Anyway, Gran, how are ya?' asked Andy, trying to change the subject.

'Tortured, tortured,' she replied, shaking her head. 'It's the mice *dirt*.'

'Are you staying with us tonight?'

'No, no, she's going home,' Mr Ryan quickly interrupted.

'I'm not goin' home to the mice *dirt*. No doubt they'll be waitin' for me. They run all over the kitchen, y'know, and leave mice *dirt* on the tabletops and the floor. They even run over the bed at night. I can feel their feet scratching on the duvet. And I can hear them in the room. I'm not going home until they've all been EXTRA-TERMINATED,' she thundered, like a homicidal Dalek.

'The mouse dirt must be the size of cow pats if she can see it. And they're obviously wearing hobnailed boots if she can hear them,' Mr Ryan said quietly to Cora. 'Come on, Mother, let's get your Granulax medicine, just in case, and get you ready for bed,' he said, taking her by the arm.

'I'm not sharing the bed with a man,' screeched an indignant Granny.

'What man?' said Mr Ryan, now truly exasperated.

'That Justin you mentioned. Justin Case. Who is he, anyway? I've never met him. Is he the extra-terminator?'

'What a day,' Andy said, as Mr Ryan manhandled his mother out of the kitchen. He breathed a sigh of relief.

'Aunty Jas will be working tomorrow and Chloe will be going to her dad's. Would you like to come back over here? Mum will be taking M'Granny out for the day and Dad's heading off early to a zoologists' conference. I'll even see if I can prise our Eoin away from the computer.'

Cora smiled. 'That would be great.'

'Good. I'll see you in the morning. Do you want me to walk back to Aunty Jasmine's with you?'

'No. No, it's fine. It's not far. And I've got Loopy. No-one will mess with me. See you in the morning, Andy.'

As they walked back towards the Callaghan house, Cora was deep in thought. 'Loop?' she said. 'Do you think the internet and *Livewire* are a big problem?'

'Well, how many people have we seen who've been completely distracted by their mobile phones?' Loopy said.

'I know. Even Mrs Ryan was checking messages from work

on her day off. And Andy is worried he's losing his brother.'

'It's not good, Cora,' said Loopy.

'Andy said they were destroying their own language. That's not good either. They could end up just using broken English and no-one will speak properly any more.' Cora sighed. 'But that's just the tip of the iceberg. This obsession with technology puts me in mind of the Skorbots and how that all turned out. Maybe we should see how the Earthlings handle things without this destructive technology, Loopy,' she mumbled as they walked along.

Her intentions were good but she had absolutely no idea of how serious the consequences would be.

'Snattery ghosts! Ye've no skin on yer face at all!'

Cora looked at Loopy. Their quiet walk was broken by loud shouting and feet stomping.

'What on Earth?' she said, scanning around for the source of the commotion.

Nothing.

She walked to the corner of the street. There she saw it.

A four-wheeled vehicle with a skull and crossbones emblem was parked by the side of the road. *Shivver me Timbers* was inscribed above the front window. On its roof was an enormous plastic cone topped with a white plastic swirl and sprinkled with what looked to Cora like hundreds of multi-coloured plastic worms.

A man in a huge white frilly shirt over black jeans stood alongside it. A black belt was wrapped around his middle and he wore a three-cornered hat. A patch covered his left eye. Red-faced, he furiously waved his fists in the air.

'Snattery ghosts! Humpy scumps,' he bellowed again.

Cora was puzzled. She wondered what a snattery ghost was. There was no sign of it, so it was obviously invisible. Was it some kind of apparition with a streaming head-cold? A sinus problem? A severe allergy?

Loopy was wondering how it could have no skin on its face. What was holding its bones in? She had fur to hold her bones in but she was pretty sure there was skin underneath.

Wide-eyed, Cora cautiously approached the man.

'Hi, is everything okay?' she asked.

He glared at the strange girl and her collie.

'Scallywags, the whole lot of them, so they are,' he said. 'They ran off and gave no blunt. By the time I got outta the van they'd abandoned ship.'

His right eye peered at her.

Cora stared back.

'I suppose ya think this is funny?' the man accused her.

'Um, no. Not at all,' she said, trying to piece together what had happened. 'Did someone steal something?'

'I'll run 'em through wi' me cutlass if I git hold o' them. Those darned picaroons have a neck like brass.'

Cora was building up quite a description of the offenders. She went over it in her head. Necks of brass, skeleton faces, humps and lots of snot. She was pretty sure she hadn't seen anyone fitting that description that day . . . or ever, come to think of it. They didn't even sound like Earthlings. She wondered which planet they were from. She was sure it wasn't SLOI, at least. There was definitely no-one fitting that description on SLOI.

'Is there anyone you can call for help?' she asked the man. Commander HardDrive had told her that some people were so evil on this planet that Earthlings had to actually pay other people to keep things under control. But she most certainly hadn't expected the villains to be children. But then, on this planet, she supposed anything was possible.

'What? Like the peelers?' The man laughed. 'Well, tis hardly the crime o' the century, now is it? What are they gonna do? Set up a hornswaggle alert? Put a photofit on TV?'

He seemed amused at his own jokes.

'Probably not,' said Cora, not having a clue what he was talking about, 'but that description you gave was very specific. I'm sure *I* would recognise them if I saw them.'

The man scratched his head and pulled the eye patch up off his left eye. This time he peered at Cora through both eyes. She certainly was a very strange girl but there was something quite likeable about her.

He shook his head, laughed, and stuck out his hand. 'I'm Billy Logan. They call me Captain Billy.'

He noticed that she glanced at the dog. He could have sworn it gave a slight nod before she shook his hand. Those thieving kids must have really screwed with his head.

'I'm Cora and this is my dog, Loopy.'

Billy liked that Cora had introduced her dog. He loved animals. He had a couple of cats himself – Pepsi and Cola.

'Does yer wee dog like ice-cream?' he asked.

'That dog will eat anything in the universe,' Cora said, laughing.

'Universe. Aye.' Billy shook his head, amused. She really was weird, this one. Catching hold of the door frame, he swung himself into the van and took an empty tub from the shelf. He filled it with smooth vanilla ice-cream from the pump dispenser and put a large swirl of strawberry sauce on top. He then handed it to Cora through the open sliding window.

Cora took it, smiled, and set it on the ground. 'There you go,

Loop,' she said.

Loopy dived in straight away, snuffling the ice-cream into her mouth as fast as she could. In fact, it was so fast that most of her face was quickly soaked with melted ice-cream, giving her a white doggy moustache and drippy whiskers.

When Cora turned back towards Billy, he handed her a large cone with scoops of strawberry, chocolate and vanilla ice-cream all crammed into it. It also had a large chocolate flake in the middle and was covered in chocolate sprinkles. He hadn't even bothered to ask if Cora liked ice-cream. He'd been doing this job for many years. He knew that children love ice-cream.

'That's by way o' apology fer this ole seadog's din,' he said. 'Must be off now. Eileen'll have m'grub ready. Nice t' meet ye both, so it is. Sorry 'bout all th' shoutin'. Good t'meet a nice kid rather than th' usual scallywags. Cheery-bye now.'

He dragged the patch back over his eye and the ice-cream van rolled off emitting a sound that to Cora's ears was like a screeching hyena. The locals would have described it as more like *I'm Forever Blowing Bubbles* being played on the chime bars by a homicidal teenager at a school concert.

She shrugged her shoulders. There were still things about these Earthlings that were completely baffling.

Cora sniffed the ice-cream. It smelled quite nice. At least she knew it wouldn't kill her – Loopy had eaten hers and she was still very much alive. In fact, she was watching Cora with eyes almost as large as the flying saucer that had brought them to this crazy place.

Cora gingerly stuck her tongue into the ice-cream and her eyes widened in wonder.

It was cold but beautifully smooth and creamy. Some of it tasted like the strawberries they'd had earlier and some tasted so different that she couldn't find words to describe it.

She gently removed the chocolate flake and took a bite. At first it was also cold on her tongue but quickly melted into a thick, yummy, sweet, velvety sensation. She could hardly believe it.

'Wow, Loopy, this is awesome,' she said reverently.

She looked down to see a wide grin and a collie head bobbing up and down in enthusiastic agreement.

Double Doors

Cora knocked on the front door of the Callaghan house. It shot open like a rocket-propelled shuttle. Two small arms circled her waist in a rugby tackle, causing her to almost topple over.

'MUM! CORA'S HERE!' Chloe's voice shrieked.

'Um, hello? Am I invisible?' said Loopy.

'Shhhhh,' hissed Chloe. 'Mum will hear you. She doesn't know you can speak. Remember?'

Loopy grinned as she scanned the hallway. 'Where's the nitwit?' she whispered.

'*Loopy* . . .' warned Cora.

'Don't call her that. It's not nice,' whispered Chloe, even though she was smiling. She knew it was true.

Skippy came wandering into the hallway. She wagged her tail, happy to see that Cora was back. She was disappointed to see that Cora had brought that Princess Lucinda back. *Loopy*, huh? *Poopy* more like. She'd been hoping Loopy would get lost again. She was like that sticky stuff on the pavement that stuck to your paws. Yeah. Gum. Bubblegum. Yeah, that was her . . . Princess Lucinda Bubblegum.

The dogs eyed each other and Skippy was sure she could hear a voice in her head saying, 'Hello, nitwit.' Of course the collie had the usual smug look on its face.

'Grrrrr,' said Skippy. Unfortunately it was the best she could do.

'Hi, Cora, come on through,' called Jasmine Callaghan's voice from the living room. 'We're so pleased you're going to stay.'

'I'm glad you're here. You always have so many adventures! You're so exciting,' said Chloe, flinging her arms wide in a dramatic manner.

'Mmm,' said Cora, 'some of them I would rather do without, though.'

'Oh dear, that sounds ominous,' said Mrs Callaghan, as the girls walked into the living room. 'What's happened?'

'Well, I met a very strange ice-cream salesman who had been attacked by something without skin,' said Cora.

Mrs Callaghan raised one eyebrow.

'Told you zombies were real!' screeched Chloe in excitement.

'Before that, Andy gave Loopy a gobstopper and –'

'Oh dear. How did she handle that?' she asked. 'You know it's not such a good idea to give sweets to dogs, don't you?'

'Oh, I didn't realise,' said Cora slightly embarrassed 'but I'll make sure she doesn't get any more'. She wondered if there was anything on this planet that didn't have some hidden danger.

'We were also ignored by people who were too busy reading messages on their phones to even notice us,' she continued, 'and Eoin and Andy had an argument that almost ended in a fight.'

Chloe's jaw dropped. She had never known her cousins to fight in all her eight years. Even Skippy looked surprised.

'That's not good,' said Mrs Callaghan, her brow furrowed.

'My words exactly,' said Cora.

'What were they fighting about?'

'*Livewire*. Apparently Eoin had been playing on it for hours and Andy was annoyed that he wouldn't come out with us.'

Chloe nodded her head. 'The internet,' she said. 'People don't want to play face to face any more. It's all they think about. I think we need Double Doors.'

Mrs Callaghan's eyebrow rose again. 'Double doors, love? How would that help?' she said.

'He could do magic.'

Cora and Mrs Callaghan exchanged looks. Neither had any idea what Chloe was talking about.

'He?' said Mrs Callaghan.

'You know, like he does in the books and the films,' Chloe said.

'Chloe, what exactly is double doors?' asked Cora.

'I can't believe you don't even know,' she said, turning her palms upwards. 'He's the wizard.'

Cora and Mrs Callaghan were still clueless.

'What wizard?' asked Mrs Callaghan.

'The one in the *Harry Potter* books. Double Doors.'

'Honey, I think you mean Dumbledore.' Mrs Callaghan was now smiling.

'That's what I said. Double Door,' said Chloe.

Amusing as it all was, and although Cora had never heard of this wizard, or even knew what a wizard was, she *was* intrigued. 'What would Dumbledore do then, Chloe?' she asked.

'Magic the internet away. And then everyone could go outside again and be happy,' Chloe said, flinging her arms in the air like an opera singer.

Sometimes eight year olds have the best ideas.

Later that night, when everyone was in bed, Cora lay awake.

'I think we need to put a stop to this ridiculous technology-obsession on this planet,' she whispered to Loopy, who was on a beanbag in the same room. 'Sloians are much smarter than Earthlings. We know how to use technology for the best.'

'Information and communication,' said Loopy.

'Exactly. We use it much more wisely, especially since the Skorbot days.'

'SLOS says that Earthlings have latched on to the dangerous things it can be used for – tracking each other, watching violent films and games, cyber-bullying and loads of other really bad things. Their addiction is going to lead to many problems and they are so caught up in it all they don't even see it coming.'

Cora shook her head sadly as Loopy described how dangerous strangers were putting false information on social media. Pretending to be another child. Just like the Skorbots had done with the Sloian children.

It made her spine crawl even just thinking about it.

'They've started on a very risky downward slope, Loopy,' she said. 'It seems that they're becoming so dependent on technology that they are missing out on the actual experience of life itself.'

'And they are losing their social skills, if they ever had any in the first place,' said Loopy scornfully.

But how could she fix this? Cora wondered. Perhaps Chloe did have a point. What had she said Dumbledore would do? Magic it away . . .

This species was obviously on the same path as the Skorbots and they couldn't even see it. Either out of ignorance or being too self-absorbed. But did they deserve a chance?

She had an idea.

She decided it was what she was going to do.

It would put a stop to it all.

If these idiots couldn't be trusted to look after themselves, then Loopy would have to do it.

'Okay, Loopy,' she said, 'here's how we're going to close those double doors.'

No Signal

The next morning Northern Ireland awoke to find the internet down. Computer and phone networks had also been blocked. There was much weeping and wailing and gnashing of teeth. Many people were highly distressed, wondering how they were going to get through the day. Some had taken to the streets, carrying placards in protest.

Teenagers were hospitalised due to mental breakdowns. Gamers everywhere were agitated and argumentative because they couldn't shoot their friends. Bakers were miffed because they couldn't put a photo of a cake they had just created on the internet. Football fans couldn't even make fun of each other when their team lost. Well, unless they actually spoke to each other . . . face to face.

It was awful.

Awfully brilliant.

Chloe was in a great mood. She didn't really care about technology. It was Sunday. Her dad was coming to take her out for the day.

Jasmine Callaghan had bought a new book the previous day and was glad of the peace and quiet.

So Cora and Loopy headed out to the Ryan house, happy with what they had done.

They had no idea of the danger that awaited them.

It had begun very early that morning – so early it was almost night. There was a loud knock on the door. Mrs Ryan was still downstairs, having just waved goodbye to her husband as he left for the long drive to the Zoological Society conference.

She thought it very odd to have visitors at that hour of the morning. It was still dark. Perhaps someone needed help.

With an uneasy feeling, she opened the door.

Two men in dark coats shoved her into the hall. They had hoods up over their heads, scarves covering their faces and guns in their hands.

'We know yer kids are here, so ye'd better do what we say or ye'll be sorry,' one of them growled, in as menacing a voice as could be managed through wool. It sounded quite nasal, as if he had a head cold.

Trying to ignore her pounding heart, Mrs Ryan attempted to be calm. 'What is it you want?' she said. Her shaky voice betrayed her.

'We'll not harm the kids if ye do what we say,' said the other man. 'Call them.'

Mrs Ryan tried to think quickly. 'Can I go up and get them?' she said. She knew M'Granny was also asleep upstairs. These men obviously did not.

'Just call them down!' demanded the first man. He gave her a hard shove towards the stairs.

Mrs Ryan knew just how loudly she'd actually have to shout to wake two teenage boys so there was a chance she could wake M'Granny. However, the old bat really was stone deaf, so maybe it was a slim chance, and she could hopefully keep her out of whatever was going on here.

She went to the first stair. Her trembling hand reached out to the banister for support. 'Eoin! Andy! Can you come down, please?' she called, as quietly as she could.

Too quietly. Nothing happened.

'Louder!' ordered the first man.

'Eoin! Andy!' Mrs Ryan's voice cracked. She heard a thump of feet on the floor and Eoin appeared at the top of the stairs. His hair was a dishevelled mess and his eyes were heavy with sleep. He had quickly heaved a red sweatshirt over his pyjamas and pulled on the nearest pair of old blue jeans that had come to hand. A stripy hem was on display at his ankle.

'Mum? What –'

He saw his mother and two hooded men.

'Andy!' His shout rocketed his brother straight out of bed.

'Down 'ere,' said the second man, beckoning them with his gun.

The boys bolted down the stairs protectively towards their mother, until one stood on each side of her.

'What's going on?' Mrs Ryan asked, now shaking like one of Chloe's birthday jellies.

'Ever heard of a tiger kidnapping?' the second man asked.

Andy's face paled. 'Touch any of my animals and I'll swear I'll kill you,' he said.

'It's not that, Andy,' Mrs Ryan said quietly, placing a shaky hand on his shoulder. 'It's about hostages. In a tiger kidnapping they hold people hostage to make sure that someone else does what they want.'

'Well, aren't you such a clever clogs?' sneered the second man.

She wondered if it was her imagination or if the man's voice really sounded familiar. 'Yes, I am,' Mrs Ryan said to the sarcastic twerp, aiming for composure. She was not about to let them know just how terrified she was. 'Is this to do with my job?'

The man used his gun to wave the family into the living room. They were all shaking now.

'Sit,' he ordered. 'Okay, you –' he continued, pointing his gun at Mrs Ryan, 'are going with him,' he nodded towards the other man, 'to the bank. You hold the safe key, don't you?'

'Yes, I'm the assistant manager, as you *obviously* know.' Mrs Ryan made another attempt at bravado. 'But you should also know it takes two keys to open the vault.'

'Aye, ole Smiley had the other one.'

Mrs Ryan swung her terrified gaze towards the man who had just spoken.

'Only he's not so smiley any more,' he said, laughing.

The other man joined in.

'What do you mean?' said Mrs Ryan, her voice rising to a squeak.

'He wouldn't give up his key, now would he. He has no family as leverage. Not like you. We had to shoot the stupid ole glype.'

He gave a spiteful laugh.

'He's dead.'

Mrs Ryan fainted to the floor.

A car quietly rolled out of the Ryan driveway.

Mrs Ryan, ashen-faced, held the steering wheel in her shaky hands. The first man sat beside her. She was still numb from the shock of hearing that her lovely boss, Mr Smiley, was dead.

They had killed him. Murdered him in cold blood.

'If anything happens to my children . . .' She tried to push the words through the tight lump sticking in her throat.

'Oh shut up, ya silly ole trout,' said the man as he peeled off his scarf and looked her in the eye.

Mrs Ryan glanced towards him. Her eyes narrowed. 'Do I know you from somewhere?' she asked. 'You look familiar. I'm sure I've seen you somewhere before.'

She was now extremely uneasy. She knew it was a very bad sign if a kidnapper took off his disguise. It meant he didn't care if she remembered his face. And that usually only ever meant one thing.

She glanced at the gun. It looked odd. Some type of plastic and metal. More like something for putting up shelves with. 'Is that thing real?' she said.

His wide grin revealed vile brown stained teeth. 'Want me to show you?' Mrs Ryan quickly shook her head. 'Then just you keep on driving. Don't worry, you won't be seeing me again,' he continued as he sniffed, wiping his nose on the back of his hand.

'What do you mean exactly by "you won't be seeing me again"?' she asked, afraid of the answer.

'Would ya ever stop with the questions!' he thundered.

Mrs Ryan decided it was wise not to push him further.

At the bank, she lowered the window. She stuck her arm out to scan her pass and open the car park barrier.

It wouldn't work.

Even old Snotty-face, as she now thought of him, couldn't argue with that. She had to park in a nearby street.

'Now I'll take yer car keys. You open up the bank,' he said in his slimy voice. He held out his hand.

Tight-lipped, Mrs Ryan slapped the car keys into Snotty-face's hand and took her work keys out of her pocket.

He followed her to the staff entrance at the side of the building and watched as she unlocked the grey lattice gate. She slid it open. Then she unlocked the heavy front doors. She pulled both doors closed without locking them. She might need an escape route . . . if she got the chance.

'Vault,' said the man.

Mrs Ryan knew he didn't mean he wanted her to run, although that was very much what she felt like doing.

Snotty-face followed her as she led the way through the main office and then through another door towards the safety deposit box vault.

She stopped. 'I only have one key. I've told you it takes two,' she said.

'An' I told you I've got that silly ole glype's key,' he said.

'Don't call him that!' Mrs Ryan raged. 'He was a good man.'

The man laughed. 'Is that a fact?' he sneered.

Mr Thing

Back at the Ryan house, the other man was making sure his scarf stayed securely on. He checked his watch. All being well, he would be getting a call from his accomplice in an hour or so to say that they were rich and it was all over.

Then he could fly off to somewhere hot and exotic, far away from this place.

He ordered the Ryan brothers to sit down and shut up. They both wished frantically that their dad was there. He would know what to do. They were frightened when they heard about Mr Smiley. Poor Mr Smiley. These evil men had just murdered him.

Eoin and Andy were staring at each other. Worried sick about their mum, they tried to read each other's minds as they wondered what to do.

An unexpected rap clattered at the front door.

The man jumped, then sidled towards the window and peered through a small gap in the still-closed blind.

'It's some wee squirt and her dog,' he whispered to the brothers. 'Stay quiet or ye'll be sorry.'

A few seconds later, the doorbell rang. Eoin and Andy tried desperately to think of how they could communicate something to Cora.

Outside, Cora stepped back from the door and looked up at the house. It was very quiet. Too quiet. Andy knew she was coming. He had told her he would be there. The blinds were closed but she'd thought the Ryans would have been up and about by now.

'They must still be asleep,' she mumbled to Loopy. 'We'll come back later.'

'It's okay. She's going now,' said the man, as Cora and Loopy wandered off.

Suddenly there was a loud clunking and shouting from the direction of the stairway. With mouths dropping open, the boys looked at each other in horror.

'M'Granny!' they chorused.

Shuffling sounds warned them that M'Granny had hobbled her way downstairs and was now staggering towards the front door.

'What's that noise? What's that noise? It's those blinkin' mice,' she wailed. 'They've blinkin' well followed me here. I knew it. Don't let them in!'

The man's mouth moved beneath the scarf but no words came out. His expression was blank. Obviously there was someone else in the house.

And mice.

He didn't like mice.

The living-room door blasted open and smacked off the inside wall like a gunshot. The man jumped almost a full metre in the air.

M'Granny stood in the doorway, wig slightly cockeyed. She hadn't put her glasses on and blinked rapidly, leaning forward to squint at Eoin and Andy as they squirmed uneasily on the sofa.

'What're you two up to now? Did y'hear those mice? They're probably doing the mice *dirt* – Oh, hello,' she said politely to the man. 'I like your beard. That must keep you very warm in the winter. And you've got a great head of black hair. Are you Mr Thing from next door? ' She spotted the gun. 'Oh, are you playing cops and robbers?' She clapped her hands in delight.

The boys groaned.

'Don't you dare touch her,' Eoin told the man through gritted teeth.

'Gran, come and sit here,' said Andy, patting the seat beside him.

Mr Thing seemed quite unsure what to do. This was an unusual hostage situation – at least, as far as he knew. He'd never actually held anyone hostage before. This was supposed to have been straight forward but it was all becoming quite complicated. Hopefully it would be over soon and he could get away from this nutty family.

'Now, aren't you going to get your granny a nice cup of tea?' M'Granny asked Andy, patting his knee.

Andy looked at Mr Thing. 'It'll keep her quiet for a bit,' he said.

'Right, go on then. Make some for all of us. I'll have milk and two sugars. Have you any biscuits?'

'No biscuits. No biscuits!' screeched M'Granny. 'Those blinkin' mice love the biscuits. After they eat the crumbs you find mice *dirt* everywhere. Mice *dirt,* it's the bane of my life, so it is.' She turned away from him. 'Andy?'

'Yes, Gran?'

'Are there any fig rolls?'

He rolled his eyes and wandered off to the kitchen.

'Don't try anything,' Mr Thing warned his retreating back, 'or she'll get the same treatment as Smiley.' He smirked to himself as he noticed Eoin's pasty face pale even further.

'Well, this is nice,' said M'Granny, settling back on the sofa for a conversation. 'Did the boys tell you about the cemetery?' she asked the gunman. She didn't wait for him to reply. 'Well, we were out for a lovely drive yesterday and there was a beautiful cemetery in the middle of the countryside. Just right there in a field. It was lovely. All on its own it was. I told my Sam I want to be buried there, so I did.' She nodded, causing her wonky wig to slide further down to one side.

A baffled Mr Thing looked at Eoin.

'It was a field of cows. Friesians, actually. She had no glasses on,' Eoin said quietly, as if that explained everything.

Mr Thing shook his head.

This family were bonkers.

Completely bonkers.

'Hurry up with that tea in there. What's keeping you?' he yelled towards the kitchen.

'Just looking for sugar,' Andy shouted back.

Andy was actually opening the cupboard where the medicines were stored. He took down Granny's bag of Granulax and dipped the spoon inside.

The door burst open and Mr Thing walked into the kitchen.

'What are you up to?' he growled.

'Um, just adding some sugar.'

'What kind of sugar is that?'

'Oh, it's, um, the only one Mum buys. It's, er, the healthy option, less calories or something,' said Andy, shrugging his shoulders. 'Mum's always trying to get us to eat more healthily.'

'Well, hurry up then,' commanded Mr Thing.

He turned and walked back to his other hostages in the living room.

Andy quickly spooned two generous heaps of Granulax into

Mr Thing's tea and gave it a speedy stir. He picked it up, then put it back down. He chucked another spoonful in for good measure before carrying the tea tray into the living room.

He handed Granny a plate of fig rolls. He really hoped they would keep her quiet. They usually got stuck under her false teeth and kept her chewing for some time. Although, that said, she would probably still keep on talking, spitting crumbs and bits of fig in all directions. Then she would start on her favourite subject again.

He handed Mr Thing his special brew and sat back down.

And waited.

He wondered just how long this would take.

As it turned out, only a few minutes. Then things seemed to happen very quickly.

First, there was a loud rumbling noise. It was so loud that even M'Granny heard it. 'Is that yer stomach, Mr Thing?' she said.

Eoin covered his face with his hands. This was surely some kind of a bad dream. A Technicolor nightmare with an all-singing, all-dancing all-crazy cast.

Mr Thing looked down at his stomach as if he couldn't quite believe it had made those noises. It gave a boisterous gurgle. He started to feel somewhat alarmed.

'I get that,' announced M'Granny. 'You shouldn't have eaten the fig rolls. You get bunged up, y'see. Then the fig rolls run through you and make your bowels loose. Then y'get the squirts.' She nodded sagely. She knew about this stuff. She had the Granulax to make her go and the Bungall to make her stop.

Mr Thing jumped up from the chair to accompanying sounds very much like a waste disposal unit. There was gurgling and fizzing, popping and whizzing. He was now very uncomfortable.

Andy's mouth twisted into strange shapes as he tried to bite his lips and keep a straight face. Eoin just looked on in disbelief and resignation.

Before they knew what was happening, Mr Thing rushed out of the room and bolted to the downstairs toilet, leaving behind an indescribably pungent whiff in the air. He was unfastening his trousers as he lurched down the hallway. He just managed to make it to the toilet in time.

Skippy would have been very impressed by the amount of special stuff he produced.

The boys leaped into action. They quickly grabbed, pulled and trailed the kitchen table and the sofa onto their sides. They piled them like an oversized Jenga outside the door of the downstairs toilet.

The door handle turned one way then the other and then shook like a supernova exploding as the prisoner tried to escape. 'Let me out right this minute!' he demanded.

M'Granny was jumping and laughing, clapping her hands again. 'Woo hoo! Cops and robbers. Ha ha! We're winning. We've trapped the baddie in the toilet. Doesn't Mr Thing know that the good guys always win?'

Eoin was about to say that Mr Thing was about to learn but he never got the chance. A resounding blast almost split their eardrums as a bullet exploded through the kitchen table and into the upright sofa at Granny's feet. It lodged itself in the stairwell in a pile of splinters and tufts of sofa stuffing. Everyone stopped dead in shock. Then they bolted quickly into the living room, Andy trailing Granny by the arm.

'What was that?' she demanded.

'Mice,' he said.

Panting heavily, the boys tried to think of what to do next

when a loud rap rattled the front door. Eoin peered through the blinds. Still dazed, he looked at Andy.

'It's Cora.' He exhaled a long breath.

Andy ran to the front door and heaved it open.

Cora was greeted by the white face and shaking body of her friend.

'Andy?' she asked. 'Are you okay? What on Earth is going on? Mr Smiley's locked in the downstairs toilet.'

Eoin appeared beside his brother. He also looked shaken. '*What?* What did you say?' he demanded.

'I was round the side of the house and saw Mr Smiley stuck halfway out of the toilet window,' Cora said. 'He told me he'd been locked in. He said you were playing a game. He asked me to sneak in and get him out, but the front door was locked.'

The brothers were stunned, speechless and confused. They wondered how this could be.

'Why would you be playing a game with your mum's boss?' she asked, deciding that Earthlings were completely weird.

M'Granny appeared in the hallway. 'It's not Mr Thing then, is it? With the beard?' she said.

'What?' said Andy.

'It was Mr Smiley all the time! Ha ha. Very clever disguise.'

Suddenly realisation dawned. He had never taken off his scarf or hood. They had never seen his face. They did not know his identity. It *was* Mr Smiley. But he was supposed to be dead!

The brothers quickly told Cora what was happening. Her jaw dropped wide open. Then it snapped into a tight line.

'Skorbot!' she said. 'Loopy, jam that window and keep him stuck tight.' She turned to the brothers. 'We need to get to the bank and get your mum now, before the robber gets away.'

'Right, we'll go,' Eoin said to Cora. 'Andy, you stay here with

M'Granny and keep her safe.'

'No. That's not fair,' raged Andy. 'She's my mum too!'

'Yes, I *know*, but someone has to look after M'Granny, and Cora and Loopy could be more help to get Mum back, if you know what I mean,' he added, nodding towards Loopy in case there was a chance that Granny might overhear. 'You're still in your pyjamas anyway, Andy. We can't waste more time. Phone the police and tell them to meet us at the bank.'

Andy's shoulders slumped. 'Okay,' he said. His face was dark, his features set in stone.

There was no way he could have known that the phone lines were dead.

The Eye of the Tiger

The bank was just over a mile away in the town centre. The children and Loopy shot through the streets like bowling balls down an alley. Suddenly Cora lurched to a halt. She could hear something. It sounded like a screeching cat.

'Do you hear that, Eoin?' she panted.

'Yeah, it's the ice-cream van.'

'Do you know Billy Logan?' she said.

'Yes, of course. Everybody knows Billy – Oh, right! Great idea,' he said, as the penny dropped.

They started to run towards the ice-cream van, scattering a number of small children like skittles. The skittles were not happy.

'Oi, watch it,' some of them shouted. It seemed that the desire for Sunday morning ice-cream was a force to be reckoned with in this place. Even early in the morning. On cold days. In the middle of winter.

'Sorry, sorry, it's an emergency,' shouted Eoin, bumping his way on through a cluster of eager children until he got to the van. 'Billy! Billy, it's a matter of life and death. You need to help us.' He leaned forward, hands on knees, trying to catch his breath.

'Ahoy there, young swashbuckler. The Cap'n don't normally

be seeing ye in such a fizz,' Billy said.

'We need to get to the bank as fast as possible.'

'By the truth?' Billy laughed. 'Tis some kind of banking emergency? On a Sunday? Surely th' bank be closed this day.'

'*Please*, Billy,' pleaded Cora, who had now caught up with Eoin. 'It's really serious but we can't explain . . . here,' she said, casting her eyes towards the circle of indignant and curious children.

Billy blinked twice while he thought. He thought this girl was a bit odd but he knew Eoin and his family very well. They were as solid as a rock – the most solid thing on the Earth. (Though if she'd know what he was thinking, Cora would have corrected him. The most solid thing on Earth is actually a metal from the platinum family – osmium. It was a stunningly beautiful lorsan colour, blueish–white on this planet's spectrum, but it could tarnish to a toxic oxide. Another irony of the planet.)

'Aye, aye, me lad. Sorry, me hearties,' said Billy, slamming the glass window shut. 'This be an emergency. The Cap'n must weigh anchor sooner than expected.' He leaped into the driver's seat.

A collective bawl of protest radiated among the children.

Eoin, Cora, and Loopy scuttled to the passenger door and bundled in beside Billy. Eoin quickly explained the morning's happenings.

'Tiger kidnapping?' Billy said. 'Shiver me timbers. And the Smiley man? Mind you, the Cap'n might just o' thought he be too sweet to be wholesome. But t' say they sent him to Davy Jones's locker? Bilge rats they be. Did ye contact th' constabulary?'

'Andy's doing it,' Eoin said. Loopy glanced at Cora but she was too busy trying to figure out what Captain Billy was saying to notice.

Billy drove as fast as he could. There was no point in asking him to be discreet. Discretion was impossible in a large ice-cream van with a skull and crossbones emblem racing full throttle down the road, vibrating the air with *I'm Forever Blowing Bubbles*.

'Can't you turn that annoying racket off?' said Eoin through a tight jaw. It was really getting on his already frayed nerves.

'Nay, lad – th' switch be jammed, so it is.'

Suddenly there was a grinding noise and the irritating melody stopped mid-*bubble*. Billy screwed up his face as he leaned his head back. 'What just happened there?' he said.

'No idea,' said Cora, patting Loopy on the head. 'It must have resolved itself somehow.'

She turned to look at Eoin but he was completely distracted. Still pale-faced, he was now wringing his hands. His breath was fast and shallow.

Cora reached out and placed her hand on his trembling shoulder. 'It'll be okay,' she promised.

She sincerely hoped that she was right.

Billy stopped the ice-cream van at the front entrance of the bank on the high street. The children and Loopy jumped out.

'Oi, hang tight, crew! Whar be ye goin'?' Billy said. 'A pair of land lubbers and a dog be not able to capture rapscallions. The Cap'n be comin' wi' ye.'

Cora and Eoin exchanged a frantic look. He was really going to get in the way. Things were very likely to happen here that an unprepared Earthling should definitely not witness.

'Billy, you can't –' Cora began.

'What mean ye "I can't", young lass? I be the Cap'n.' He puffed out his chest.

'We need you to stay here in case the kidnapper tries to escape this way,' said Eoin, gesturing towards the main entrance. He didn't mention that the front door was likely still locked and that the employees only ever used the side entrance. 'We'll just check the side door and then by that time the police will be here. Okay?'

'I be not liking this one bit.' The frown lines already on Billy's forehead tightened further.

'Honestly, it'll be fine,' said Eoin. 'We're just going to take a quick peek and then we'll come right back. The police are on their way. We'll need you to take charge.'

That was different. It was a Captain's place to take charge. And these kids had the dog on their side. He peered at Loopy again. A pair of collie eyes boldly held his gaze. *Aye, she'd give ye a right bite that one, so she would,* he decided.

'All right, but ye need t' be quick,' he said, straightening up to his full height now he was in charge. 'Just a look, mind ye – 'n be sure t' steer clear o' danger. Get back t' th' vessel fast.'

Cora and Loopy followed Eoin to the side entrance. The metal lattice gate across the door had been pulled closed but when Eoin tried it, he found it was unlocked. He slid it open and tested the main door with the palm of his hand. It opened inwards.

Four feet and four paws crept inside. Eoin wondered what kind of kidnapper would leave a door unlocked. Someone very sure of himself? An idiot? Someone wanting to make a quick getaway? It all seemed very odd. But then this whole thing was very odd.

Eoin knew the general layout of the bank. He had been there before a few times with his mum when she called in on days off. He knew that the side entrance opened into a small corridor, which they tiptoed along. Then came the staff room with its small kitchen on one side and cloakroom on the other. Another heavy door stood between the staff room and the customer desks.

He knew that the security vault was situated at the back of the tellers' section in a big room behind yet another heavy door but he had never been in there before.

For extra security, none of those areas had windows. The only windows were right at the front of the bank alongside the front entrance where they'd left Billy. Thankfully he wouldn't see them going against the captain's orders.

'Cora,' Eoin whispered when they reached in the staff room. 'The biggest problem is opening the internal door. This one opens behind the customers' section. You have to go through it to get to the vault. There's no other way. That's probably where they are. We don't know how many of them there are and it's keypad access only and I don't know the code!' The tone of his voice rose in panic.

The children stared at at each other with wide eyes. Seconds passed as hope melted away.

'Loopy?' breathed Cora, hardly daring to hope.

Loopy stepped forward. She gazed at the keypad. Nothing. She gave it a hard stare. Nothing. She frowned at it. Nothing.

'What are you doing, Loopy?' whispered Cora frantically.

'I can't quite seem to link up to the system for some reason. This is really weird.' Eoin's body was buzzing with adrenaline, ready for action but nothing was happening. His stomach began to churn. He felt sick. They'd come so far. How were they going to get in to save his mum? A sob broke and pushed its way up his throat.

Suddenly, as Loopy's eyes bore into them, the keys flashed up and down faster than a shower of rain in Belfast. The heavy door gave a click. Loopy leaned her body against the door, encouraging it to open a few millimetres at a time. Slowly . . . Slowly . . . Silently she opened it enough to let the children through.

'How did you –' whispered Cora

'Fingerprints on the keypad,' said Loopy. 'I had to try 46,021 combinations before I got the right one. Six, four, eight, three, seven, hash.'

Eoin snatched a pencil off the nearest desk and jammed it under the door. He put a finger to his lips and pointed towards another heavy door at the back of the room. The thick rubber tiles allowed the children to creep along, though Eoin thought the robbers must surely hear his heart beating – it pounded like a hammer trying to break down the wall of his chest. He was doing his best to breathe normally but he knew he was almost hyperventilating. He hoped his mum was okay. He wondered what was taking the police so long. He wished again that his dad was there. *Well, he isn't,* Eoin reminded himself. Eoin would just have to do his best. He was glad his friends were there, though.

The children put their ears to the vault door and heard the muffled sound of raised voices. They couldn't make out what the voices were saying but Eoin recognised his mother's voice. He breathed a quiet sigh of relief, even though he knew from her tone that she was exasperated, and trying hard to keep her patience.

There was some kind of an argument. It became more intense. Both voices became raised and the children looked at each other in horror as they picked up snatches of what was said.

'How can ye not open it, ya stupid woman?' yelled the robber. He gave a loud sniff, then a mucous-filled cough. 'Don't give me that drivel about the computer not working. It's just another ruse. Do ya think I'm completely stupid?'

Mrs Ryan snorted in answer to his question before going on, 'Look, I'm telling you that the computer system that opens this door isn't working.' She enunciated each word very carefully as if speaking to an idiot.

'Why not?'

'I don't know. I'm not an internet engineer,' she screeched back at him. She punctuated this with a few other words to add weight to her argument. This revolting mucous man was asking her to do the impossible.

Eoin's eyes narrowed as he gave Cora a distressed look. 'She's losing it,' he whispered.

Cora nodded. 'I'm sure I recognise that other voice,' she whispered back. 'And . . . um, Eoin? Your mum is telling the truth. The computer systems are actually all down.'

'What? How do you know that?'

'Um . . .'

Their short conversation was interrupted by Mrs Ryan's loud scream. 'Let go of me, you oaf!'

'If ye don't open that door right now I'm going to phone my mucker and tell him to shoot those namby-pamby kids.'

'SKORBOT!' screamed Cora, as she launched herself through the door like a nuclear missile.

Loopy leaped into action. She would defend Cora – always. She soared through the air. Her satellite navigation system was the best in the universe. Her aim was perfect. She knocked the kidnapper to the ground.

But somehow he still held tightly to the gun.

That should not have happened.

Then Loopy remembered. The satellites weren't working. She was the one who'd meddled with them. It took only one second for her to unblock the jamming signal to get them back on line. But it was one second too long.

The kidnapper fired.

The Giant Slushy

A streak of light flashed across the room.

'MUM!' screamed Eoin in horror as he watched his mother shrink right before his eyes. Her skin turned grey and she began to sprout hair all over her body. Her face shifted into a pointed shape with a little wet pink nose and whiskers.

Two triangle-shaped ears popped up on her head. Her arms morphed into tiny legs with pink claws at the same time as a long pink tail appeared.

A startled Mrs Ryan looked round at the tail and gave a squeak of alarm. She then skittered off across the floor and squeezed under a skirting board.

'Mum!' cried Eoin. 'No. Oh no!' Nausea rushed up his throat. He didn't know what to do. A mouse? Had his mum just turned into a mouse? Eoin scanned the room. And where had she gone?

Cora's gaze swung back to Loopy. She could see the collie had the gunman mostly under control.

A furious Loopy had bitten hard on the gunman's arm. She knew it wasn't necessary. She'd already immobilised him by this stage, but she just wanted to bite him. She wanted to bite him hard. Tearing through the flesh, she found there was no blood. Her teeth clattered on metal but she held it firm.

Cora ran along the edges of the room, calling for Mrs Ryan.

Eoin turned to the gunman. 'What have you done?' he yelled, just as he realised the man had no mask.

Snufflebot!' Eoin roared, but stopped short when something glinted on the man's body. A metal wrist? He looked again. Yes. There was metal, and bare wires that even Loopy couldn't bite through.

Cora's head spun to the gunman, as the truth dawned. 'Snufflebot,' she repeated. 'SnuffleBOT!'

'ROMhat, RAMcoat, Snuffle BOT. Why didn't I notice before?' Eoin exclaimed. He banged his hand against the side of his head. 'Is he some kind of robot, Cora? What is this *thing*?'

'Skorbot!' hissed Cora in disbelief.

No. No. It couldn't be.

A Skorbot?

Here?

On this planet?

Snufflebot used the distraction to spring to his feet. He was fast. And strong. He heaved Loopy aside and pointed the gun at her head, ripping another piece of flesh off his arm in the process. 'Your police cells couldn't hold a Skorbot.' He leaned forward as he hissed at Eoin through a twisted mouth.

'Eoin, go, go find your mum,' Cora said. Her voice was measured, her eyes never left Snufflebot's face.

Snufflebot looked her in the eye. 'Go ahead and try. It would give me great pleasure to shoot this skanky mutt,' he said. His lips were pulled back, revealing a brown-stained row of miniature metal daggers.

'I can't Cora,' wailed Eoin. 'He'll shoot Loopy.' His heart twisted inside his chest. How could he choose between this kind girl's best friend and his own mother? The sick feeling rose in his throat. He was going to have to.

'Try it,' said Loopy to Snufflebot.

Snufflebot's hand was smashed to the side as she flashed through the air like a NASA rocket lifting off from Kennedy Space Centre.

He fired at Loopy. The laser ray did a U-turn in mid-air and veered into the Skorbot's foot. The smell of singed metal filled the air.

'You darned Sloians and your gravity control!' he yelled. 'I should have destroyed that WooFi collar when I had the chance.'

He shouted some words in a language they couldn't understand and then, like an express train straight out of hell, he bolted for the door.

Things were also happening on the high street.

Having waited a few minutes, Captain Billy decided he was going to phone the police to find out what was taking them so long. Unable to get a signal on his mobile phone, he wandered further up the street. Still no signal. So he wandered round the side of the bank – the opposite side to the staff entrance – waving his phone about, searching for a signal.

At the same time there were loud screeches, much shrieking and hilarity as a bicycle veered helter-skelter towards the bank. A bicycle wasn't an unusual sight on a Sunday morning, but this one had a trailer attached – essentially a red seat on two wheels with a plastic canopy in case of rain – which was always a good idea in this part of the world.

On it sat an elderly lady laughing like a spitting llama.

'Hold on to yer wig, Gran,' shouted Andy, as he did the bicycle equivalent of an emergency stop outside the bank, wondering why there was an ice-cream van parked there.

He had tried to phone the police but the line was dead. So, remembering his mum's bicycle with the trailer in the garage, he decided to lend a hand at ground zero. He had even remembered to get dressed. The only downside was that he had to bring M'Granny. She created enough havoc when you were trying to keep an eye on her, never mind when she was left on her own, let alone with a gunman locked in the downstairs toilet.

'Wee-ee! That was *GREAT*!' M'Granny laughed as she wriggled herself out of the trailer.

'Oh look, Gran – ice-cream. Why don't you get in there and get us all some lovely ice-cream, eh?' said Andy, manhandling her into the van with a gentle shove. 'I'll be back in a minute.'

Like Eoin, he knew where the staff entrance was. He bolted round the side of the building and reached the door just as a figure came hurtling in the opposite direction, smacking into him and slamming him hard against the wall.

'Snufflebot?' Andy said, staring after the figure. Now he was confused. What was Snufflebot doing there? Wasn't he in police custody?

The door flew open again, and Cora and Loopy raced out. Cora promptly grabbed Andy by the arm.

'Andy, help! He's getting away!'

'Snufflebot?' said Andy, still dazed. 'Where's Mum and Eoin?'

'They're still inside,' Cora panted. 'We need to stop Snufflebot. He's a Skorbot! We mustn't let him escape.'

'A Skorbot?' Andy could hardly believe his ears.

They sprinted after him, towards the high street where Loopy was close on his heels.

'How can we stop a Skorbot, Loopy?' Cora shouted.

'I've punctured his arm and he shot his own foot. He has exposed electronics. We can short-circuit him.'

'How?' yelled Cora.

'Water. Any kind of water!' Loopy bounded on. She launched herself at the Skorbot in a spectacular leap, knocking him to the ground. They fell in a heap, tumbling and rolling in front of the ice-cream van.

'Where can we get water?' Andy shouted. He frantically looked around for a fire hydrant, or a random hose just lying around.

'Yoo-hoo! This has got water in it,' shouted M'Granny in delight as she waved the slushy-maker pump. She figured they must be playing cops and robbers again. This was all so much fun!

'Switch it on, Gran. Quick!' shouted Andy. 'Get him!'

There was a loud whoosh as an eruption of blue juice, water and ice was launched through the window of the ice-cream van as M'Granny wrestled the hose like a thrashing python.

Giant slushy waves washed over the still rolling Snufflebot and Loopy. Nothing happened. Loopy wrestled hard, barely able to hold him down.

It wasn't working.

'Why isn't it working?' shouted Cora, her voice bordering on hysteria. This was all her fault. Then the penny dropped. 'Loopy move!'

Loopy rolled to one side. She'd been lying on his exposed circuits.

Straight away there was loud hissing, fizzling and bubbling. Steam and smoke began to rise from Snufflebot's arm and foot.

Loopy got to her feet and stepped aside, shaking off icy lumps of blue slushy.

A pungent smell of burning cyborg resistors filled the air as Snufflebot began to short-circuit. White froth bubbled from his mouth as his arms and legs juddered like a tractor crossing a cattle grid. There was more hissing, pinging and sparking.

With mouths wide open, the children guarded their prey. The circuitry in Snufflebot's wrist began to decompose. The effect spread along the rest of his body, quickly turning him into a pile of blue goo right in front of their eyes. Very soon, all that remained was a slushy-soaked laser gun. It short-circuited then exploded.

Only the wail of a distant siren broke through their awe.

Suddenly, Eoin came thundering up the street, carrying something small and furry in his hands.

'Is that a mouse?' said Andy.

'Mice? Mice?' screeched M'Granny.

Before anyone could stop her, she turned the slushy hose on Eoin, drenching him to the skin.

Startled, he dropped Mrs Ryan and she plummeted to the ground. M'Granny continued to hose blue slushy over everything in sight, covering the children and Mrs Ryan. 'Did I get it? Did I get it?'

The drenched mouse gave a loud squeak as it suddenly began to change. Growing larger, it became pink and evolved into the shape of a woman.

'Mum?' said a completely baffled Andy.

'You can turn it off now, Gran,' said Eoin, staring at the gooey mess. 'The mouse has gone.'

'What?' she screeched, turning towards him. The blue tidal wave sloshed over him.

'Gran!' he yelled. 'Turn it off!'

It finally stopped. The machine was empty.

'Did we win?' said M'Granny.

'We surely did,' he said, shaking his head in disbelief.

Finally managing to get a signal, Billy Logan phoned 999 and the police and an ambulance were dispatched to the Bank.

Strange hissing noises and raised voices reached his ears as he ran back to the entrance. And there was a very strange smell of scorched metal.

He saw an ambulance followed closely by a police car, turn into the high street.

Andy was there with M'Granny. Billy knew M'Granny. Everybody knew M'Granny. It looked like she had gone barmy. She was waving the slushy-maker hose and there was a serious heap of blue icy mess on the pavement.

Mrs Ryan was there – drenched – and Andy, his brother Eoin and the odd girl. All of them were dripping blue slushy. There was also some kind of mangled toy gun at their feet.

'What on Earth just happened here?' Billy said, his usual pirate talk forgotten. 'I was only away a couple of minutes, so I was.'

Andy could hardly get his head around what had happened. He wondered if this was some kind of a dream. McGranny's fast action with the slushy had saved them all. Really? Well, either that or he was going insane.

Police swarmed into the bank like a bucket of marbles poured over the floor. Andy just about remembered to tell them there was another gunman locked in their home in the downstairs toilet.

Officers were dispatched straight away to the Ryan house. Riley Smiley quickly surrendered. He knew he had no choice. He came out with his hands up and his trousers down.

The police officer who questioned Mrs Ryan was quite concerned about her. She was unable to remember a lot of what had happened, but what she did mumble seemed to be about robots and flying dogs. She even said something about a dog talking and people speaking in a foreign language, so the officer motioned to the ambulance crew.

'Shock, I expect,' said the paramedic, 'but it's best if she comes with us to the hospital to get checked out properly'.

Mrs Ryan was feeling very strange as she was helped into the back of the ambulance. She seemed to have a craving for cheese. She wrinkled her nose. It was all very odd as she didn't particularly like cheese.

The police cordoned off the area as it was now a crime scene. A police officer took Eoin into the reception area to take his statement. He told Eoin that they had already put a call out for his dad and he would be with them soon. Eoin was still shaking as he told them about Snufflebot and how they could get his address from his dad's records at the zoo. He didn't tell them that they wouldn't find Snufflebot there, just that he'd disappeared. No-one would find him anywhere. This time he was really gone. He just wished he'd been there to see the end of the scumbag.

The brothers went in the ambulance with their mum and M'Granny was left with Cora and Loopy in the care of a police officer until they could get a police canine car to take them home.

'I need to make this very clear to you,' the police office told Cora in a stern voice. 'What you did was very dangerous. You should never ever tackle gunmen. You know that, young lady.' Her voice softened. 'But you have all been extraordinarily brave.'

'We had no option. We were the only ones who could help. Mrs Ryan was in great danger,' Cora replied.

The police officer said she understood that they couldn't get through to the police as there seemed to have been some kind of strange satellite failure earlier that morning.

'I'm really sorry Snufflebot got away. I do hope you find him soon,' said Cora, batting her eyelids.

As the police officer closed her notebook she could have sworn she saw the collie smirk.

Home

M'Granny was beside herself with excitement as she was assisted into the back of the police car where Cora and Loopy were already waiting. She couldn't believe how everyone was making this game feel so realistic.

'Oh look, a police uniform. Where did you get that, son? It's very realistic,' she said. She thought the police officer was quite tall for a youngster at play, but then Eoin was also tall. You couldn't really tell who was what age these days, but she was very excited that they were still playing the cops and robbers game.

'I hosed the baddies with blue slushy *and* I hosed the giant mouse,' M'Granny announced. 'The dog told me to.'

'Yes, that's lovely, dear. A great help,' said the police officer. He had noticed the ice-cream van and the huge heap of blue icy mess in the high street. Now he knew who was responsible, it really didn't surprise him in the least.

The officer drove M'Granny, Cora and Loopy back to the Ryan house. He had decided that he couldn't leave a young girl in charge of the barmy granny, so decided to stay with them to wait for an appropriate adult to arrive. He sincerely hoped there was actually such a thing as an appropriate adult in this nutty family.

Andy and Eoin had gone in the ambulance with their mum.

They found their Aunt Jasmine and Chloe already at the hospital as their dad had phoned Jasmine when he had been contacted by the police. Thankfully Mr Ryan had been stuck in a traffic jam on the motorway and had been able to follow the police car along the hard shoulder. As his wife was whisked off for scans he was already talking urgently with the doctors.

Eoin's vacant eyes had a red tinge. He was worried sick about some terrible lingering effect of the Skorbot ray and he couldn't even confide in anyone. Aunt Jasmine gave him a hug and Chloe, wordless for a change, took hold of his hand.

The waiting room doors swung open and Mr Ryan dashed in.

Chloe hugged her own mother tightly as she watched Andy and Eoin run to their dad. They might have acted like tough teenagers but sometimes everyone just needs their dad.

Sam Ryan pulled his boys close. He told his sons that the doctor said their mother was fine and they would be able to see her very shortly. 'Thank goodness you're okay. I could have lost you all today,' he said. His throat was tight and his eyes glistened with moisture.

At that, both boys gave in to their overwhelming emotions.

A desperate sob at the back of Andy's dry throat finally pushed its way though. Their dad was here. It was going to be okay.

Eoin's heavy head rested hard against his father's shoulder. They didn't have to be superhero alien-robot fighters any more. They could just be ordinary teenagers.

'The police told me what happened,' said Mr Ryan. His eyes were dark and there was a black look on his face. 'I can't believe that Smiley scumbag pretended to be dead. What a disgustingly cruel thing to do to your mum. And holding children ransom? I hope I don't see him or that Snufflebot ever again. I won't be responsible for my actions.' His voice was gruff. 'I can't believe we actually had him working for us. What kind of lowlife is he anyway?'

'Skorbot,' Eoin mumbled as he looked at his brother. Andy gave a slight nod. The boys even embraced each other. Awkwardly.

The doors opened and the doctor entered. She said they could go in to see Mrs Ryan, though not all at once. She brought Mr Ryan and the boys in first.

Mrs Ryan had an intravenous line in her arm giving her a sedative. Wires attached to her chest monitored her pulse and heart rate. She was sleeping peacefully. Her husband and sons stayed only briefly. The doctor said she needed her rest.

Then it was her sister and niece's turn.

Jasmine Callaghan looked at her sister. She felt like things were happening around her but she was disconnected from them. Like it was a dream – a nightmare. She supposed it was her brain's way of protecting her from being overwhelmed. She wrapped her arms around her little daughter who clung to her tightly, tearful and frightened.

Sam Ryan couldn't describe whether he was upset, angry or relieved. He guessed it was a mixture of everything. His emotions were all over the place. However, one thing he did know. He would be eternally grateful to the boys' young friend and her brave companion who, by all accounts, had saved his wife's life.

The exhausted family piled into Mrs Callaghan's car.

When they arrived home, Mr Ryan actually managed to laugh out loud when M'Granny told him her version of events. Robots? Talking dogs? Giant mice? She really was bonkers. But at least she had temporarily forgotten about her favourite subject.

The Report

Just after midnight, when Chloe and her mum had fallen into a deep sleep, Cora and Loopy silently opened the door and crept a long way from the house. They headed to the woods at the back of the Ryan house. Eventually they came to a clearing big enough for Loopy to allow SLOS to direct the small, two-person spaceship down from orbit. Its invisibility screen was still in place so as soon as Cora and Loopy stepped on board, they couldn't be seen.

The Super Loop Operating System automatically came online. Emperor RAMcoat, the Great Galaxian himself, appeared. Looking at his dark hair and dark eyes, Cora realised just how much he resembled his sister. Her mother. Cora's eyes blurred. Eoin and Andy had almost lost their mother today. The day before, she had almost lost Loopy. Her quest for revenge had almost cost Cora her best friend.

'Cora, my dear, I didn't expect to hear from you until you got back. Is everything all right?' said Emperor RAMcoat. His eyes were soft and his voice was gentle. Cora looked so young and fragile. RAMcoat had known this would be a difficult mission for her but she had been so angry he'd had no alternative. He knew she had needed to make this journey, physically and emotionally, but three years ago she was just too young.

'Yes, its fine, Uncle. Nothing to worry about. Is Commander

HardDrive around?'

'We can get her online,' he said. 'Is it for your report? You always did get your work done early,' he said, smiling. 'We have always been proud of you. And not only because you are intelligent,' he added, 'but simply because you are you.'

With a loud click, the screen divided in two and another face appeared. A voice boomed across the light years. 'HardDrive here.'

'Commander,' said the Galaxian, 'Cora is ready to give her report.'

'What did you find?' the Commander asked, always quick to get to the point, although her voice had softened a little.

'Okay,' said Cora. She took a deep breath. 'Here goes.'

She described what it was like when she arrived on this far-flung planet – the feelings of isolation and dread. She told them about the bullies who attacked her and tried to destroy her hat for no reason.

'I could see straightaway that Earthlings were nasty and vile – as I expected. Exactly as we expected,' she said. 'I met bad people. Really bad people. Evil. Nasty. Selfish. There were dognappers who kidnapped Loopy, just to make money. Thinking that an animal was a commodity that could be bought and sold.'

'Just one reason they need to be destroyed. Those people are so greedy and incredibly stupid. They'll kill us all,' Commander HardDrive thundered.

'Hush, Commander,' said the Galaxian gently. 'I have a feeling Cora's not finished yet.'

'Far from it,' Cora said, her face flushing slightly.

She described the delightful Chloe and the comical Skippy. She spoke of the wonderful animals in the zoo, the species that they didn't have on SLOI. She told them about the Ryan family. She talked about their kindness, love and compassion for each other and the animal kingdom. She told them how the children had helped her save Loopy from the dognappers.

'That's when things began to change,' she said. 'I came to Earth angry, looking for revenge. I was prepared to destroy them all. But, Uncle, I learned that the humans had crashed the satellite into the asteroid to deflect it from its original path – a path that would have destroyed their planet.'

Her voice cracked like splitting wood as realisation pushed its way through. 'We'd have done the same thing, wouldn't we?'

There was silence.

Static was all that could be heard.

Eventually a subdued voice was heard.

'I can answer that,' said the Commander. She looked down at her hands. 'We would. We would have. We've just been lucky enough never to have had to.'

With her lips held tightly together, Cora gave a slight nod. 'I thought so,' she whispered.

After another moment of silence, Cora straightened up, pulled back her shoulders and raised her eyebrows. 'We also found a Skorbot,' she stated simply.

'What?' chorused RAMcoat and HardDrive in stereo.

'The dognapper was a Skorbot. It seems he'd lived on this planet for quite a while. They've even taken on the worst of the human traits now. Selfishness and greed. Money seems to be all some of them think about. We thought he was going to kill us all. He threatened to kill our friends after kidnapping their mother. All so that he could make money. Sadly, she shook her head. 'But don't worry, Uncle, Loopy and I dealt with him with the help of the Ryan brothers and M'Granny. We'll definitely not be seeing him again.'

'Who's M'Granny?' asked RAMcoat.

'Oh that's a whole story on its own.' Cora laughed. 'I'll tell you another time.'

'Well, Cora, it sounds as though you learned a lot on your journey,' said Emperor RAMcoat, 'with all of its dangerous bends.'

'Uncle? I need to ask you something.' Cora stroked her eyebrow. 'Um, did you send me to this particular place on Earth on purpose?'

The Galaxian smiled. 'The Land of Ire? They're an angry people, the Irish. But under the bluster you'll find kind hearts.'

'You knew?' she said.

'I knew.'

'You knew my journey, Uncle, before I came here? But how did you know?'

'I'm the Galaxian. I've travelled all over the galaxy. I've seen many things.'

'So why didn't you send me three years ago?'

'You were so young when you lost your parents Cora. You needed to blame someone. It was part of the grieving process. But you were not ready for the journey at that time. We had to wait until you were wise enough to unravel it for yourself.'

He looked affectionately at his beloved niece. 'Are you ready to come home now, Cora?' he asked.

'That's the funny thing, Uncle,' she said. 'I feel like I am home.'

He smiled. As if he'd already known that too.

As the whirring sound faded into the distance, a young girl stood on the grass in the cold, damp air. A cool wind picked at the ends of her golden-brown hair that was beginning to frizz in the damp. She smiled down at the collie standing by her side.

'Come on, Loopy,' she said. 'Let's go home.'

Together they walked back to the Callaghan house.

Finding Meaning

At the Ryan house the next morning, Mr Ryan was on the phone with the hospital. He turned to the children, and through misty eyes he told them that Mrs Ryan was doing well. She was to be allowed home as soon as Mr Ryan could come for her, and was currently sitting up in bed, having tea and toast.

Eoin took Cora aside. 'You saved my mum's life, Cora,' he said. 'We could never have destroyed Snufflebot without your and Loopy's quick thinking and bravery. I don't know how I'll ever be able to thank you.'

Her eyes glistened. 'I'm so sorry, Eoin. Part of it was my fault. I got Loopy to block the computer systems and phone lines.' She hung her head. 'I made some awful mistakes even though I was trying to help.'

'No need to be sorry. I know that after what you've been through yourself you would never put my mum, or anyone else, in danger.'

An image flitted through Cora's mind of Piddler in the Irish Sea, before Eoin continued.

'You've helped me put some things in perspective, you know? Realising what's really important,' he said.

'Friends and family?'

They grinned at each other.

'Hey, guess what?' he said. 'I also found out something else interesting.'

'Oh?' said Cora.

'Remember how I said your name sounded familiar?'

'Uh-huh. I thought it was because you recognised the ROM in ROMhat.'

'Well, it's something more than that too. I'm doing Irish language at school and the penny finally dropped.'

'Penny?' she said.

'Your name – Cora Romhat?' he said. 'Have you ever wondered what it means in the Irish language?'

Cora looked at him in puzzlement. 'The Irish language?' Her lexicon buzzed. 'You mean Gaelic? Um, no. I've never even thought of it,' she said.

'Well, I didn't recognise it at first as the words are pronounced "Kura Rowet", but they're spelled Cora Romhat. It means, *dangerous bends ahead.*'

Cora began to laugh.

'Isn't that ironic?' he asked.

Cora shook her head. 'No, Eoin, it's not. And to be honest, I'm not even sure it's a coincidence.'

Back at her new home in the Callaghan house, Cora reflected on her dangerous journey. She thought about the people she'd met. If she had continued to focus only on the bad, she could easily have given the order to destroy them all. But it was almost as if there were two types of humanoid on this planet.

Could that be possible? she wondered. Perhaps half of them didn't come from Earth . . . Might they be Skorbots? Or part-Skorbot? She had to admit, it seemed possible. That would explain their obsession with technology. Maybe that was how to tell the difference.

No. She realised that couldn't be right. There was Eoin. He was almost lured into a technology addiction and he was one of the best people she'd met.

So, really, it wasn't possible to separate people into groups. You couldn't tell anything about people from where they lived or what they looked like. Mr Smiley was a perfect example of that too.

Her idea to shut down the technology had facilitated disasters that she could never have imagined. It had almost cost Mrs Ryan her life. Cora felt really guilty about that. She was thankful that Loopy had only shut it down locally, although who knew how many people she'd put at risk. Technology had immeasurable benefits. She'd learned a harsh lesson. Things were never just black or white.

Technology itself was not a bad thing. It was really the people who were using it who were the problem.

She still felt she had to do something. But what could she do?

She looked at the collie lying peacefully beside her, happy on her own couch once more. She'd give Loopy something to do while they stayed on Earth. She could monitor the internet and *Livewire.* That would work.

She wondered if they should issue a warning to the Earthlings . . .

When your system runs slow . . .

When your internet crashes . . .

When your phone cuts out . . .

When your technology fails . . .

It's for your own good.

It's Loopy.

She's watching you.

No, Cora decided. ***Let them figure it out for themselves.***

Also by Elaine Abrol

The Space Hopper

A short story about Andy Ryan and his gran. When Andy loses his homework he finds himself transported to another planet - the one where all the lost things go. Really? Yes indeed, there is such a place! He meets Flapper and Splasher who say they want to help him. But do they really? Or have they got their own agenda? But that's not all... there's an even bigger shock for Andy. Something totally unexpected and mindblowing...

Printed in Poland
by Amazon Fulfillment
Poland Sp. z o.o., Wrocław